ROSS'S GAP

Also by G. Clifton Wisler

Antelope Springs

ROSS'S GAP

G. Clifton Wisler

Walker and Company
New York

First published in the United States of America in 1988 by the Walker Publishing Company, Inc.

Published simultaneously in Canada by Thomas Allen & Son Canada, Limited, Markham, Ontario.

Library of Congress Cataloging-in-Publication Data

Wisler, G. Clifton.
  Ross's Gap / by G. Clifton Wisler.
  ISBN 0-8027-4081-2
  I. Title.
PS3573.I877R6 1988   813'.54—dc19   87-37373

Printed in the United States of America

10 9 8 7 6 5 4 3 2 1

To all those who have walked the high places above the Brazos and shared the fiery light of summer campfires—especially those who shared the well-remembered tales with the boy I was and the man I have come to be—*Ross's Gap* is dedicated.

ROSS'S GAP

Prologue

PALO Pinto County straddles the Brazos River in western Texas some 200 miles due north of San Antonio and a little less than 70 miles south of the Red River. The land there is hard, rock-strewn, and cut by wicked ravines choked with nettle and cactus. The plain to the east gives way in the west to the Palo Pinto Mountains, a series of low ridges of speckled stone dotted by the sun-scorched frames of mesquite and juniper trees.

The early Spanish explorers who visited the place named it for that peculiar grayish-brown stone, which they thought resembled a painted stick. It is found nowhere else. To the natives who first made their homes along the high cliffs above the river, that stone marked the boundaries of the land set aside for them by the sky spirits. The Kiowas and Comanches, who arrived later, came first to hunt the buffalo. They stayed to make their camps along the great river.

Following the wars with Mexico, which assured Texas first its independence and later its boundaries, white men came to the country of the painted stick. First there were the ranchers and farmers, who sought land granted by the government as payment for military service. The Overland Stage crossed the Brazos near the mouth of Bluff Creek, where the high canyon walls gave way to a gentler incline.

For a time, bitter conflict flared as the Indians sought to hold off the encroaching fingers of the Texans. The U.S. Army established Ft. Belknap just to the north, in Young County, as a base for operations against the hostiles. For a time an uneasy peace existed. A reservation was established for the Indians along the northern shore of the river. But

1

although the more pacified tribes, the Caddos and Tonkawas, accepted reservation life, most of the Comanches never abandoned their free ways of hunting and raiding. Hundreds of steers and horses were taken from ranches each year.

The Texans decided enough was enough. Just as the cliff dwellers had given way to the Comanches, the reservation tribes were uprooted and sent north into the Indian Nations before the outbreak of the Civil War. The old post at Belknap was closed, and the teamsters and traders, who had seen it all, headed west to hunt the buffalo or tried their hand at raising horses and cattle on the spotted hillsides of Palo Pinto.

The outbreak of war between the gray-clad soldiers of the Southern Confederacy and their bluecoat brothers to the north provided an opportunity for the Comanches and their allies to increase their raiding. Flames raged across the Texas frontier. By 1864 Palo Pinto County was virtually depopulated. But the close of the war and the return of the cavalry to the frontier signalled the end of Comanche invincibility. Band after band of raiders was hunted down and either trapped or forced by starvation to accept the fate of life on the reservation.

The summer of 1874 witnessed the final moment of independence for the Comanches. The buffalo herds were dying off, killed by groups of hunters with long-range Sharps rifles and rapid-firing Winchesters, who in a single day could sweep an entire generation of the huge woollies from the earth. The last of the great chiefs, Quannah Parker, struggled hopelessly to avoid the determined columns of bluecoat cavalry led by Colonel Ranald Mackenzie. At Palo Duro Canyon on the Red River, Quannah managed to lead his people to safety. But their lodges, winter food, clothing, and even their ponies were destroyed by Mackenzie. The gnawing ache of hunger and cold finally forced all but a few defiant warriors to lay down their arms and surrender.

It was the end of an era. Soon railroads would crisscross

the Texas landscape. Barbed wire would slice up the range. Schools and churches would appear in towns, and roads would take the place of horse trails.

A new day was dawning. To the farmers and ranchers who had withstood the heat and the cold, the scourge of Comanche raids, and the oppression of carpetbagger judges, it was the long-awaited hour of redemption. To others, the old frontiersmen and buffalo hunters and the few Indians whose eyes filled with a final trace of defiance, it was a time of passing, of giving way to the new season even as winter yields to spring.

CHAPTER 1

IT was autumn, the season of change, and the winds that swept southward across the rolling hills of west Texas carried with them a hint of transition. Even as splashes of orange and scarlet invaded the deep green forests of oak and willow, the tranquility that had settled over the small farms and ranches along the Brazos was disturbed by the pounding of hoofbeats and the blare of bugles.

Mackenzie's on the move again, Carter Ross thought as he gazed across the shallow riverbed at the thin column of Yankee cavalry. It wasn't the first time. Ever since Mackenzie had arrived at Fort Richardson back in the spring of '71, the cavalry had been actively scouting out parties of Kiowas and Comanches. More than once Carter had happened upon the aftermath of one of Mackenzie's skirmishes—a few burned lodges, a handful of sad-eyed women and children surrounded by a detachment of soldiers. Nearby several corpses stared blankly at the midday sun.

"Soon the Comanches'll be gone, too, just like the buffalo," Carter said to himself sadly as he stared at the cavalrymen vanishing into a cloud of dust the other side of Fortune Bend. It was a disquieting thought, the passing of the Comanches. Not so many years before, Carter had thought no power on earth could sweep those wild horsemen from the hills and valleys watered by the Brazos. But then who could have imagined the buffalo would disappear?

Carter turned back from the river and examined the spotted hills that made up his home. At least the land didn't change. Ioni Creek still wound its way along the base of Antelope Mountain as it had from the moment old Walt

4

Harper and Carter's father, Charleston Ross, had first splashed their way across the Brazos in '49 and staked the place out as their own. The Ionis themselves were long gone, of course, like the ancients who'd put their burial platforms high upon the cliffs.

"It's the nature of the world for one people to pass on and another to follow," Walt had said more than once. That hadn't seemed so important back when Carter was fourteen and hunting deer with the old man after his father's death. Now, at thirty-two, Carter'd seen enough changes for one lifetime.

He glanced over at the creek where his wife, Hope, sat with little Rachel. Upstream the boys splashed and laughed their way through the long September afternoon. Beyond them the cattle and horses grazed, hemmed in by the rugged slopes of the mountains and the wide waters of the Brazos. The only escape route was the quarter-mile gap that stood between Antelope Mountain and its sister ridge, which had once been known as Wolf Hill. After Carter's father died, it had been renamed Ross Mountain.

Before the war, Carter and his half brother Johnny had built a rail fence across the gap in order to keep their stock from wandering off. Now the fence served notice that visitors were neither needed nor welcome. Carter's family lived scarcely more than four miles from the fledgling town of Palo Pinto, so when company was sought, he would load the family into a wagon and ride into town.

Such visits were rare. When supplies were needed, Carter generally led a string of horses to market in Weatherford or sent word to the army procurement officers at Ft. Richardson up at Jacksboro or Ft. Griffin out on the Clear Fork of the Brazos. Barter was easily enough arranged. A Ross pony brought a high price at auction, and Carter's four years of riding with Nathan Bedford Forrest's Confederate cavalry through Tennessee and Mississippi had taught him more than a little about what the troopers looked for in a remount.

"Don't see how a man who wore the gray could do business with them Yanks, Carter Ross," his neighbor, Ben Copeland, had complained.

"Easy enough," Carter had answered. "Yank greenbacks pay Yank taxes. Most everything else I need's on the land."

Yes, the land, Carter thought, smiling. After his father's death, Carter had inherited everything east to Wolf Branch, west to where the Jowell spread began, north to the Brazos, and south to Walt's cabin atop Antelope Mountain. One day Walt's holdings would pass to Johnny. That was understood. But the old man was tough as buckskin and would likely see another dozen snows.

"This is a good place," Carter's father had said when they'd ventured into the valley that first time back in '49 when Major Charleston Ross had left the army to take a Comanche wife. "We'll have solitude here."

The major had only lived seven years there before the chills of a hard winter had choked the life out of him. Old Walt Harper, who had served the major as orderly sergeant a dozen years, had looked after Carter and six-year-old Johnny.

That was a long time ago, Carter thought, remembering how he'd chased his little brown-skinned, dark-haired brother through the creek, how the two of them had ridden half-wild mustangs into the camp of Johnny's uncle, Nighthawk. Yes, it seemed a century had passed. First there had been the war. For a while after his return, Carter had seen his brother from time to time, always in the pale light of a new moon, tall and lean with eyes bright as the stars. But now, not even Walt saw Johnny.

"Keep him safe," Carter whispered, glancing at the blazing sun overhead. It was as close to a prayer as Carter could speak anymore. The memory of his brother's glowing face was replaced by a vision of Mackenzie's cavalry and the recollection of the cold, lifeless eyes of the men Carter had seen more than once stretched out beside the smoldering ashes of a Comanche lodge.

"The sooner every Comanche's wiped from the face of the earth, the better," he'd heard another neighbor, Jasper Farrell, say on more than one occasion.

Unless one of them's your brother, Carter wanted to answer, and you can remember holding onto his trembling shoulders as Walt Harper shoveled dirt over your father. Unless that Comanche's bonded to you by the blood that flows through the both of you, even as it does through your own children.

Carter shivered. There was a sudden chill to the air, and he walked toward the creek. The four boys continued to chase each other through the stream. Carter sat down on a rock and watched.

Some things didn't seem to change at all. It didn't seem possible it was twenty years ago Carter had chased Johnny through that very same creek. Wasn't it yesterday they'd trapped their first mustang pony down in Doan Hollow? Carter smiled as he remembered. All that had happened when the world was young. Now the creek belonged to his sons, even as it would one day to theirs.

Carter studied the boys. Brady was the oldest at thirteen, already growing tall and straight as a Ross should. The boy had his mother's auburn hair and quiet, serious nature.

John Tyler, though—he was born of the twilight sky, as old Walt liked to say. At twelve he was thin and wiry, with hair that grew almost white in the summer sun. J. T. was the leader, whether for good or bad, and the others followed, usually to their regret. The boy was half horse, could ride from one end of the ranch to the other by midmorning and still find time to discover some new bit of mischief to get into.

The little ones, Nathan and Richmond, had been born after the war and were somehow dearer for it. Each was a smaller version of John Tyler, even as J. T. often seemed the second coming of his father. But neither Nathan, at seven, nor Richmond, three years younger, possessed J. T.'s way-wardness or Brady's dour nature, either, for that matter.

"You weren't five years absent from their lives," Hope reminded him from time to time. "It was never in Brady's nature to roam far from home pasture, but J. T., well, he'll never accept a tight rein now."

More than once Hope had remarked what a trial it was to raise such a wild child. But beneath it all Carter knew she delighted in J. T.'s love of life in a way only a mother could.

For his part, Carter found little Rachel a joy. The girl was terribly spoiled by her brothers and old Walt. She was never without playmates or attention, and her mother always seemed able to find a bit of yellow calico for a new dress. The amber hair that seemed to impart the devil's own nature to J. T. bestowed on Rachel a brand of angelic innocence, at least in the eye of her father.

"Why do white men build houses of stone?" Nighthawk once asked Carter. "Why do they write their names upon the land? Don't they know we pass upon the earth as the wind, staying only so long as the sky spirits decide?"

As Carter gazed at Hope and the children, he realized the answer was, For them. We do it for them.

Carter walked slowly toward the creek, waving his hand overhead to attract the boys' attention.

"It's time you boys climbed on out of there," he called, waving the boys to the shore.

"But, Pa," J. T. complained.

"Out, now!" Carter commanded, and J. T. led his brothers to the bank.

"You're cold," Hope said as she rested her head on Carter's shoulder. "I hope you're not catching a fever."

"No, I'm all right," he assured her.

Hope placed Rachel's tiny hand in Carter's larger one, then turned her attention to Nathan and Richmond. By that time Brady and J. T. had managed to shake half the creek off their bodies and wriggle into faded overalls.

"I used to think boys were a blessing," Hope said as she struggled to dry Nathan's hair.

"Wild as summer corn," Carter grumbled, lifting Rachel up onto his shoulder. "What do you think of those crazy boys, huh, little flower?"

Rachel just shook her head, and Carter laughed.

"Least I don't wet my britches no more," Richmond hollered at the top of his voice.

"Anymore," Hope corrected him. "You're a year older than your sister at any rate, Richmond Ross. And scarcely any taller."

The other boys laughed, and Richmond's face flashed scarlet.

"Don't let 'em annoy you, son," Carter said, swinging an arm around Richmond's bare shoulder and turning toward the cabin.

"Sure's not easy bein' little," Richmond grumbled.

"No, it's not," Carter agreed. But then being taller or older didn't make life much easier.

While the boys fetched water from the creek and chopped kindling for the supper fire, Carter walked to the edge of the cabin porch and stared off into the distance. The dust from Mackenzie's column had been swallowed by the spotted hills to the west. Once again the Rosses were left in the security that isolation brought.

"Why so solemn?" Hope asked, intertwining her fingers with Carter's.

"Oh, just thinking," he told her.

"About Johnny?"

Carter nodded, and Hope squeezed his hand.

"I recall how he came to stay with us when you rode off to soldier," she said. "Why, he wasn't but what, J. T.'s age? Still, he was determined to look after us, see we had meat, see that the little ones didn't fall prey to wolves. The Indians left us in peace, too, even when the Jowells and Crandalls were being burned out regularly. Then when you returned, he was off like a startled rabbit, back to the plains."

"It's the Comanche way to return a favor. I looked to his needs when Pa died. He saw it his obligation to see you got on."

"What will happen to him now, Carter?"

"I don't know," Carter said, sighing. "I trust he's safe, but who can tell? The world's changing."

"Agnes Slocum was by again."

"Was she?"

"Seems Reverend Hollings has begun his school at the Methodist Meeting House in Palo Pinto."

"Oh?"

"I thought maybe it's time we sent the boys, Brady and J. T. anyway. Maybe Nathan as well."

"No," Carter said, releasing her hand.

"Carter, why not? You can't ignore the neighbors forever."

"No, Hope. All our boys need to know can be learned right here. You can teach them to read the Bible and those history books your brother sent out. Brady already writes a fair hand. They know their cyphers."

"There's more to life than reading and writing."

"Sure, there is. They'll learn that from me. I'll teach 'em the land, where to find the curing herbs, which roots you can eat, and what springs still flow in the dry months."

"They need to be around other children."

"Why? Look at me, Hope. Do I seem all that different from men in town? I wasn't around other children for years while Pa was enlisted. After Ma died I traveled wherever Pa was stationed, instead of staying back in Carolina with my older brother Andrew. I'm no worse for it than most, am I?"

"No."

"You know, when Pa died, I was only fourteen. Walt wrote Pa's family back in Carolina, asked if they'd send for me and Johnny. Know what they said?"

"That Texas would be a more appropriate place for you."

"Those were the words, not the meaning. The Rosses of South Carolina didn't want a six-year-old halfbreed or a kid who'd been living with Indians. When I was in Alabama, I happened upon my brother's regiment. I sent word I was in Selma. I got a kindly note saying Andrew thought it best not to renew old acquaintances. He sent money, Hope. Money!"

"I know," she said, resting her head on his shoulder. "But that was a long time ago. We can't wall ourselves off from the rest of the world forever. The children are part of that world."

"But I'm not."

"You could be," she said, stroking his forehead. "You served in the army. You pay your taxes. There are lots of people in this county who think highly of Carter Ross."

"And even more who can't forget my father married a Comanche, that I lived with Nighthawk's band, that even now I've got a brother out there with Quannah Parker."

"Some of those people lost relatives in Indian raids. It's hard for them, Carter. Once they get to know us . . ."

"You're wrong, Hope. I know. I've tried before. There's a world of difference between us."

"That's what bridges are for. It wasn't accidental your father picked out this spot. There's a pass through the mountains. It makes it easy for people to come here, for us to go out."

Yes, Carter thought. Ross's Gap. But one of the first things he and Johnny had done after their father's death was build a fence across that gap.

"We could start by attending Sunday meeting," Hope suggested. "Would it be so hard?"

"Yes," Carter told her. "But if you're set in your mind to do it, go ahead."

"And you'll come, too?"

"I can't, Hope. I've done too much praying in my lifetime. It doesn't work, not for me. God's sent me a hard path to follow, and no circuit preacher's going to make it easier."

She held him tightly, and Carter felt some of the pain fade. But he was still glad of the fence across the gap, of the wide waters of the Brazos, which kept neighbors at a distance.

That night after supper Carter heard the muffled sound of a single pony on the sandy trail leading to the cabin. He took a shotgun from the gun rack and stepped into the doorway.

"Hello up there, Carter Ross," a familiar voice called. "It's just a weary old horse trader."

Carter lowered the barrel of his shotgun and smiled at the approaching figure of Walter Harper. The old man was closing in on his sixty-fifth year now, and what hair remained on his head was white and gray. He had nigh as many wrinkles on his forehead as there were stars in the sky, but his eyes remained bright and active, and he sat on his horse with the same ease with which he'd once led a cavalry charge.

"What brings you out this way, Walt?" Carter asked, taking the reins from the old man's hand.

"Oh, just wanted some company."

"You saw Mackenzie's column."

"Sad to say I did. Got a bit of a visit from their scouts."

"Jasper Farrell?"

"Him and three Tonkawas. Tonkawas I can tolerate well enough, but that Farrell's not worth a duck egg."

"Seemed like a big column."

"Regimental strength. After Quannah Parker, they say. Might be they'll catch him this time. Farrell says they got wind of some Comanchero traders out west. Might be a meeting."

"That's common enough."

"Surely, but that Mackenzie's not your regular Yankee horse soldier. He's got the eye for business. He might just catch up with Quannah and have it out."

"Could be, Walt. That why you came over?"

"Well, I took to feeling melancholy. Need some company just now. Any around?"

"Sure," Carter said, leading the way inside the cabin. "Four boys who love to hear your stories and a little girl who likes to sit on an old man's lap."

Walt grinned and followed Carter through the house and out the back door. There, spread out on cloth blankets on the wooden porch, which would one day be the cabin's fourth room, were the children.

"How's my little flower?" Walt asked when Rachel wrapped her small arms around one knee.

"Got any candy?" the child asked.

Walt shook his head no, but produced a bright red cardinal's feather for the girl instead. The boys gathered around, and the old cavalryman began spinning a tale about fighting off a ferocious bear back in the old days. After an appropriately gory climax, Walt left the boys to their dreams, passed a sleeping Rachel to her mother, and motioned Carter off down the hillside.

"Sky seems strange," the old man observed.

"Trace of red to the twilight, too," Carter recalled.

"And the moon," Walt said, pointing to the haze that clothed the bright silver sphere overhead. "It's a hunter's moon. Good for seeking out coons or deer."

"Or Comanches."

"Buffalo's all gone from the county. Few left up north of Ft. Griffin, but they won't last long. It's the end of the old ways."

"Change. It always comes."

"I'll find it hard this time, son."

"Me, too," Carter said quietly.

"But there's one who'll have it harder."

"Yes," Carter agreed, thinking of his brother off riding with Quannah, enjoying the final hours as a hunter before Mackenzie's cavalry turned him into the quarry.

"They say there's still country up north where a man can hunt all day and never see another white face."

"No, I hear there's a railroad into Santa Fe now, another one on its way to Canada."

"Times've changed."

"Happens," Carter said sadly. "So what will Johnny do? Ride till Mackenzie's bluecoats cut him down?"

"Might come home," Walt said. Carter could tell it was more wish than belief.

"He'd be welcome," Carter said. "It's been a long time since we've raced our horses down the creek."

"Crandall's taking half his cows up to the railhead this year. Aims to get rich."

"I've got what I need right here, Walt," Carter said, nodding toward his family.

"Hope you can hold on to it all, son," Walt said. "Storm's coming, and that's for sure. Always comes with the hunter's moon."

Carter followed the old man around the cabin and watched him ride off. In a way it was good to know someone else sensed the strangeness in the air. But it brought no comfort to know another man would find it equally hard to adapt to the coming changes.

It will be difficult to live like the others, Carter thought as he returned to the cabin. He wasn't sure he'd ever be ready to ride to Sunday meeting or watch the boys head to town each day for school. Yes, it would be hard to accept the changes. But as he stared through the window at the shrouded moon, he knew for Johnny it would be nigh impossible.

CHAPTER 2

SEPTEMBER came and went, and the winds of October cast the veiled hunter's moon into memory. The leaves on the white oaks and willows down by the river grew brittle and fell slowly, somberly to the ground. Soon it would be winter, that season of death that so often swept away the young and the infirm, the old and the weak.

Carter Ross never greeted those gray, chill, late autumn mornings with the same fervor as an April sunrise or July afternoon. Perhaps it was the ache old wounds sent through his joints or the memory of yellowing wheatfields littered with dead friends a decade before. But that was war, and men had died in April and July as well. Down among the boulders and ravines below the Brazos, it seemed death came with the snows, was cold as ice and near as hard.

"You can't worry yourself to death over Johnny," Hope told him almost daily, it seemed. "There's nothing you can do."

The thought provided no comfort. Being powerless to change the world around him led a man to despair. Only Hope's soft touch, the sparkle of her walnut eyes, and the way the sunbeams danced on her auburn hair brought warmth to his heart. Yes, the world around him was shuddering with the impact of transformation. But in the end, the most precious part of his world—Hope and the children—remained constant.

There was Johnny, though.

Often at night Carter would find himself staring off into the distance, imagining his brother riding with Nighthawk across the buffalo valleys, howling as he had at ten, his long brown hair flying behind him as he struck some lumbering beast with a killing lance.

The buffalo were near gone now, of course, and the Comanches fought with rifles and pistols. Johnny wasn't ten anymore, either. Carter knew that. In truth, Nighthawk's band was likely fleeing columns of Mackenzie's cavalry, heading out into the vast emptiness of the Llano Estacado, the staked plains. There they would be, cold and desperate, with only meager winter stores of dried meat to sustain themselves. Whenever the midnight image of haggard warriors and their scarecrow women and children haunted Carter, he would shudder himself awake and stare at the plank ceiling overhead.

"You can't worry yourself over Johnny," Hope would whisper again. And Carter would try to sweep the terrible nightmare from his mind. He rarely managed it.

During the daytime, he kept busy working the stock. The cattle had a habit of wandering up the creek in autumn, and with the days growing shorter, the boys often lacked enough time after their lessons to nudge the animals homeward. More often than not Carter found himself chasing strays from the rocky ravines and hillsides.

Then, too, he had a pair of promising mustangs in the corral, ready to be gentled so that they might be sold at market next month. He enjoyed working with the horses, found the toil and pain a distraction from a world that seemed to have gone crazy.

"You figure next year maybe we'll drive some steers up to the railhead, Pa?" Brady asked as he rode beside his father not far from where Ioni Creek emptied into the river.

"Don't know it'd be worth it," Carter grumbled. "We could round up five hundred head. Some lose a quarter on the way. There'd be the hiring of extra hands, and the markets in Dodge City have fallen of late."

"Thirty dollars a head, Pa," Brady said, grinning. "That's what the Copelands got last summer. They only had a hundred or so head, though. If we took five hundred, well, that'd be fifteen thousand dollars! Ma could buy all the hats she could wear. We could fix up the house some, even add that extra room."

"Tired of bunking with brothers, huh?"

"Oh, it's not so much that," Brady said, gazing westward. "It would be nice to have some peace now and then, though,"

"Guess it would. Maybe we'll add that room come spring. Old Walt will help, and I know where there's a fine stand of oaks up Ross Mountain."

"What about the cattle, Pa?"

"We'll see, son," Carter promised. From the youngster's heavy frown, Carter suspected Brady knew it wasn't likely.

What does he know of Kansas? Carter asked himself. All he's heard is talk of greenbacks and fancy houses. No one's talked of Kiowa raiders and Yankee rustlers, of stampede and disease.

Carter wished it were possible to build a wall fifty feet high around the ranch, to shield his family from that world beyond the gap. It wasn't. Keeping the boys from Reverend Hollings's schoolhouse or avoiding Sunday meetings failed to keep bits and pieces of the world from breaking through. The Copeland boys, Hadley and Moss, were fond of swimming at Fortune Bend, and J. T. rode out to the stage station on the Jowell place to sell bits of carved wood or squares of his mother's cornbread. More often than not the boy would return with a Jacksboro newspaper and the latest gossip from the lips of old Putnam Daniels, the station boss.

"Pa, look there!" Brady called, pointing across the river at a swirling cloud of dust.

Carter shook himself alert and followed the dust. Too orderly to be Indians, he told himself, and too slow to be a storm's blow. From the west? It wouldn't be a supply train. No, more likely one of Mackenzie's companies, bound back for the comforts of the post at Lost Creek. Ft. Richardson wasn't any kind of paradise, but it sure beat the Llano!

"Soldiers," Carter mumbled as he began to pick the first blue-shirted riders from out of the dust. "Back from chasing Comanches."

"Yankees," Brady said sourly. "Figure Uncle Johnny whipped 'em, Pa?"

"That's best not thought of," Carter warned as the soldiers turned toward the river. "I'm sure Nighthawk would just as soon stay well clear of Mackenzie. That's one soldier that's hard to shake once he gets on your trail. So I've heard."

"They're coming right along to the river," Brady declared. "We going to meet with 'em?"

Carter had not the least inclination. He still bore the marks of a Yank saber on his leg, and though he found the cavalry fair men to trade with, he saw no reason to share their camp. But as the soldiers split their column, Carter changed his mind. Five wagons rolled along behind the horse soldiers. Peering out of the open beds of the first two were a dozen gaunt-faced women. Some held small children or cradled babies in their thin arms. Behind them a boy or two stared hatefully at the troopers.

"They're Indians," Brady whispered.

Kiowas, Carter observed by the style of their hair and the pattern of their dress.

"Must be forty or fifty of 'em," Brady went on. "It's a whole village, Pa. Can we go down and talk with 'em?"

"You best go along to the house," Carter said, nodding in that direction. "I'll find out what's happened."

"Ah, Pa."

"Brady?"

"I never saw this many Indians altogether, not even when Uncle Johnny took me out to hunt with Nighthawk."

Carter frowned. As a boy, he'd walked through Comanche camps of fifty, even a hundred lodges. That hadn't been a good day's ride from where Brady sat atop his horse that very minute. The world was changing, yes, indeed.

"Come along, son," Carter said, waving Brady along. "Let's go see what's afoot."

The cavalrymen were preoccupied with tending their weary mounts and pitching tents. They were accustomed to visits by the farmers and ranchers that scratched out a living along the Brazos, and they paid no mind to Carter Ross and his thirteen-year-old son. Carter passed a pair of sentries, then gave a nod to a Michigan sergeant named Sloan who had recently accepted delivery of half a dozen remounts.

"Been some doin's, Ross," the sergeant remarked as he wiped his dusty face with a wet cloth. "We did ourselves proud."

Carter gazed at the sad-eyed wretches piling out of the wagons. Who could be proud of waging war against women? The few males over ten were manacled. The whole bunch were skeleton thin, and Carter judged most would die before winter ceased her torments.

"Well, if it isn't Carter Ross!" Jasper Farrell then bellowed from behind the second wagon. The grizzled old buffalo hider and sometime army scout grinned wickedly as he pulled a young Kiowa girl out of the wagon. He slung a small bundle onto the ground beside her, then booted a small boy who attempted to intercede.

"I see you haven't lost your affection for Kiowas," Carter remarked as he climbed down from his horse.

"You got enough love for these Indians to make up for the balance of the county, Ross," Farrell replied, spitting tobacco juice onto the ground near Carter's boot. "Never will understand how a white man can turn so soft in the head!"

Carter turned away from Farrell and studied the captives. Their eyes were empty, lifeless. Here it was October, and the children stood barefoot and near naked. Where were the buffalo robes, the buckskin moccasins? Where were the men? What could have brought such despair to a proud people?

The same question filled Brady's wide eyes. The boy moved among the captives, whispering to them in the language learned from an uncle now a world away. The Kiowas drew away, though. Their eyes revealed their mistrust.

"Seems your boy there's not got your way with Indians," Farrell said, laughing. "Well, likely doesn't matter. Won't be any Indians 'round come spring. Those that don't throw in their cards'll clearly starve. Or get pulled in like these ones."

"Some won't," Carter declared. "Quannah knows the Llano. Then there's Lone Wolf's Kiowas."

"These are some of Lone Wolf's band here," Farrell said, grinning. "As for Quannah, he's surely worn through his moccasins by now."

"What?"

"Guess you don't know what's happened," Farrell went on. "Well, sit yourself down and listen to the tale of Palo Duro."

Carter sat on a rock and motioned Brady over beside him. The two sat in stunned silence as Jasper Farrell related the story of the fall campaign to clear west Texas of hostile Indians.

"Was a clever man put old Ranald Mackenzie on Quannah Parker's trail," Farrell began. "Another soldier might've kept to the old way of chasin' Comanches in spring and summer, when their horses are fat on green grass and the sun is high and bright. Ole Mac, he did his share of chasin' in summer, then kept after 'em in September. We were chasin' shadows out on the Llano for a month. Then Bill Gratt and I caught sight of some Comanchero traders. We brought a couple of companies along later on and had ourselves a chat with those traders. They were mighty helpful. They told us right where to find Quannah and his friends."

"I never knew Comancheros to give a white man, much less a cavalry colonel, the time of day," Carter commented. "And to betray Quannah!"

"Well, I'll confess we encouraged 'em some," Farrell said, the grin on his face widening. "Set 'em on fire, we did. Comanchero will talk a blue streak when his legs're burnin'."

Carter frowned. Behind Farrell's smile was a ruthlessness,

and as the scout continued his tale, the extent of that ruthlessness became all too clear.

"Comancheros agreed to meet Quannah at Palo Duro Canyon, near Tule Creek, way up on the high plains," Farrell explained. "We burned up the blankets and flour the traders were bringin', stowed away the cartridges and the rifles, then set those bandits afoot in hopes the buzzards'd have 'em for supper 'round November. Then we kept their meeting with Quannah.

"Was somethin' to see, Ross! Comanches, Kiowas, bands of this tribe and that, all camped down on the creek at the base of the canyon. You couldn't ask for a better trap. We swept down on 'em like a whirlwind, shootin' and hollerin'! Wasn't much of a fight. Those who could scramble away did. We shot the rest of 'em. Took the whole pony herd."

"Oh?" Carter asked, gazing at the soldiers. Their mounts were weary, and few showed the distinctive traces of mustang bloodlines.

"Didn't keep 'em, you understand," Farrell explained. "Quannah's an old hand at stealin' mounts. Mac had us take 'em and shoot the whole bunch. Smell like to knock us over, all that dead horseflesh in the September sun. But it's finished the raids, Ross. And I can't help feelin' my brother Fitz'll rest easier knowin' his murderers are finally feelin' some of the pain he knew."

Carter gazed at the captives again. He saw in their faces the end of the frontier, the death of the tribes. He'd met Mackenzie a year or so back at Ft. Griffin. The colonel didn't seem the type to slaughter horses. What sort of man could order a thousand ponies shot? It couldn't be possible.

Sergeant Sloan confirmed the story, though. At least most of it.

"Wasn't a battle, of course," the sergeant declared. "I been in battle, and this was a badlands ambush, pure and simple. Truth is we didn't lick 'em, either. We didn't find but a handful of bodies when it was all done with. We took the village, though, and besides shootin' the ponies, we burned up all the winter meat, the lodgepoles, the skins and blankets, even the cradleboards of the babies.

"All you got to do is look at those kids, at the women to know it's all over. We caught this bunch out in the open. Their men put up a bit of a fight, but they shot up their ammunition fast, and we had an easy time of it. Come over here and have a look."

Carter followed the sergeant down the trail. A wagon lay a quarter mile from camp. By the time Carter approached to within a hundred yards, he understood why it had been left there. The smell was overpowering. Inside, stacked like so many sticks of firewood, rested eleven corpses. Stripped naked, rotting from exposure, the bodies nauseated Carter Ross.

"Captain's proof he's done his job," Sergeant Sloan explained. "I'd left 'em something to cover themselves, but the boys picked 'em clean. Wanted souvenirs, I suppose, and the captain didn't stop 'em. Farrell and his scouts would've done worse, but I guess even the captain's got a little respect for the dead. You can't tell now, but I'll bet half of those Kiowas wasn't as old as your youngster. They fought hard, but that's not enough, is it?"

"If it was, you'd never taken Richmond," Carter boasted.

"Not pretty to look at, this campaign," Sloan said, leading the way back toward the river. "But I've seen Comanches before, and I've buried men that sampled their handiwork. This had to be done. I just wish . . ."

"I know," Carter said, pausing as Sloan rubbed his hand across his face. "Men ought to fight a war out in the open, and the women and kids should be left be. Wasn't that way in Tennessee, you know."

"Or Virginia. I rode with Phil Sheridan when he burned the Shenandoah Valley."

"Sergeant, you figure your captain might be tired? Maybe I could talk to him, get him to rest a day or so. I'll bring over some beeves. Maybe we can put some meat into the bellies of those kids. As it is, most of 'em'll never get through the winter."

"I know," Sloan confessed. "I'll talk to Captain Kendall. Call him colonel. He still wears the eagles he won in the war. Might help turn him to your argument."

Carter nodded, then followed Sloan past the other wagons, through the huddled captives, and along to the soldier camp.

"Colonel Kendall," Sloan said, motioning toward Carter, "this is Mr. Ross. He supplies remounts to the regiment, and he's got an offer of sorts."

"I don't buy horses," Kendall said, sadly eyeing his animals. "Bad as I need remounts, you'll have to contract 'em at Griffin."

"Yes, sir," Carter said, nodding. "I don't have any ready just now anyway. What I was thinking about was bringing over a couple of steers for your outfit. The men look in need of a rest, and those Indians are near starved."

"We couldn't pay you."

"Don't recall asking anything in turn," Carter said. "Colonel, I've campaigned myself, and I know what a couple of months in the saddle does to a man. You may be in a rush to report in, but if not, I offer you my meager hospitality."

"I've heard of you, Ross," the captain said, examining Carter carefully. "Farrell here says you were raised by Comanches."

"My father married one," Carter explained. "He was a full major in the old army, and when he died, I lived with my stepmother's people for a time. I make no secret of the fact. It's well known hereabouts."

"And you rode with Forrest."

"That's known, too. I don't look upon the time fondly, for that war was bitter hard on all of us. But I saw it a duty, and I never shied from my responsibilities."

"And what are these Kiowas to you?" Kendall asked. "I've watched your boy. He speaks their tongue."

"When I was off in Tennessee, my brother Johnny looked after my family."

"His brother is the one who's half Comanche," Farrell declared, stepping from behind a wagon into full view. " 'Course there's no such thing. A man's Comanche or he's not."

"I wasn't talking to you, Farrell," Carter said icily. "You take the offer how you will, Colonel."

"I'd find it hard to trust a man who's sympathetic to my enemies," Kendall explained.

"Say I am," Carter suggested. "Aren't you? Those aren't mounted warriors out to scalp you, Colonel. There are little kids who won't see their next birthday if somebody doesn't do something."

"They'll tend 'em at the reservation," Kendall declared.

"Up in the Nations? No, winter's just a time to die up there. Ever been to Ft. Supply or the new post at Sill? Tribes just wither and die there. At least let these people have a brief moment when their bellies are full. And besides, your soldiers look worn through. I'll wager a square meal wouldn't be lost on them, either."

"All right, Ross, but I'll have your word you won't abet any escape."

"You have it," Carter promised, wondering how in creation those pathetic wretches could slip past a dozen sentries or wander far on hollow stomachs and wasted limbs. Any with life still in their eyes were shackled like criminals.

"Brady!" Carter called then, and the boy trotted over. "Let's go drive a pair of steers over for these folks. A milk cow for the children, too."

"Pa, is it true about the lodges, the horses?" Brady asked.

"I'd say so," Carter admitted as he led the way to their own mounts.

"How will the Comanches get through winter?"

Carter shook his head and mounted his horse. They both

knew there was little chance of surviving winter on the Llano naked, afoot, alone. And they shared the haunting vision of Johnny Ross stumbling across a snow-covered plain, singing a death chant as the world itself wept.

CHAPTER 3

THE captive Kiowas passed two nights across Fortune Bend on the Brazos before Captain Kendall set himself in motion one again. As the wind whined down from the north, growing ever harsher as November arrived, Carter wondered how many of the sad, weary faces still looked upon the world of the living. When snow fell a week later, he tried not to picture the shivering bodies and forlorn faces.

More and more his thoughts turned to Johnny. He found himself praying on moonless nights that a God who had seldom taken pity on the Rosses might for once smile upon the gaunt brother who likely wandered the Llano with what remained of the Kwahadi Comanches. Even if Quannah admitted defeat and trudged his way to the reservation north of the Red River, Johnny would not go.

"There's no place for me on a reservation," he'd said once. "Nor here either. I'm not white, not Comanche. Out on the plains it doesn't matter so much. I'm free there."

Johnny was right, Carter thought. People like Reverend Hollings were around, trying to reform you. There'd be Jasper Farrells bearing grudges for events decades old. But Mackenzie's patrols rode the Llano, and Carter feared that what freedom remained on the plains was fleeting.

That early November snow proved a prelude to as hard a winter as Carter could recall. Snowdrifts eight inches deep swept the hills, and Ioni Creek actually froze solid for three days. Even when the sun finally appeared, it was only to duck in and out of gray clouds.

"That's what comes of praying," Carter told old Walt

Harper. "I ask God to look after Johnny, and He sends a foot of snow to freeze him to death."

"If your mama could hear you!" Walt scolded. "You got so much sense you know God's business, do you? Why, snow isn't particular who it freezes, and it's for blame sure Mackenzie's taken to his winter quarters. Johnny, why he knows how to make a shelter, where to hunt and camp. He was born to the Llano, same as you, Carter boy, and he's got no fear of things he can understand."

Neither do I, Carter thought. But who can comprehend a world gone mad, cavalrymen shooting horses, or the Llano Estacado without buffalo or Comanches?

Walt felt it, too. Three days later when Carter took Brady and J. T. out to cut wood for the old man, Walt sat in his solitary chair by the fireplace and spoke of better times.

"Sometimes I wonder where the time's gone," Walt said, taking a pipe from the mantle and carefully filling the bowl with tobacco. "Seems just yesterday I rode into Nighthawk's camp with you and Johnny, you holding onto my back and him riding on my saddle horn. The both of you together weren't but the size of a good sliver of Tennessee pine. There was Nighthawk, tall and straight and all the time giving me the cold eye."

"It would've been easier for you if you hadn't worn those old cavalry britches," Carter said, laughing at the recollection.

"Ah, those were the only pair of pants that didn't have holes in the seat. Ed Widler used to sew 'em up for me, but when we left the army, I was on my own."

"Nighthawk took us in," Carter whispered as he gazed out the window. Nighthawk was young then himself. He had yet to earn the reputation of a feared warrior or a great hunter. Comanche kinship obliged him to open his heart and his lodge to Johnny, but no blood bound Carter to the Comanches. Some hinted a white boy, especially one so fair, would bring trouble. Nighthawk had merely laughed, pulled Carter from Walt's horse and clasped the boy to his side.

"You remember it all, don't you?" Walt asked.

"Those were good times, maybe the best I've known."

"You grew tall eating buffalo in Nighthawk's camp."

"Much more than that," Carter declared. "He taught me to rely on myself, how to draw others close to my heart. It's hard losing so much of your family so young. I saw boys in the war all hard-boiled and hollow-hearted."

"Yeah, he even found a place for an iron-headed fool like me."

"And now he's out there in the cold with Johnny."

"Most likely."

"Or worse."

The boys brought in two armloads of oak logs then, and Carter helped Brady stack them beside the hearth. Walt went on talking of Nighthawk, and as the boys warmed themselves, they pleaded for a story.

"That's for your pa to do," Walt said, puffing on his pipe.

"Please, Pa," J. T. begged, settling on the floor beside Carter.

"You know your ma's against high tales and such foolishness," Carter told them. "There's work to be done."

"Tell us, please," Brady added. "I know Ma doesn't like you to scare Nate and Rich, but they're not here. You never tell us about when you lived with Nighthawk, and Uncle Johnny's not been here for months."

"They should know," Walt said, nodding toward the distant unknown. "The hawk would have his best days remembered, even if it has to be by a pair of scruffy river rats like these two."

Carter nodded, then began telling them of hunting an old black bear in Doan's Hollow. Fear and high drama combined to steal the boys' attention. They hung on their father's every word. And when the bear breathed its last, even old Walt sighed.

"You know," Carter said in conclusion, "I believe that's the one and only bear I ever saw in this country."

"Could be it was the last one," Brady sadly mumbled.

"Or maybe it wasn't a bear at all," J. T. suggested. "Uncle Johnny says sometimes the spirits send young warriors a test."

Carter nodded. Nighthawk had said as much when they'd been unable to locate the huge beast that next day. More likely something dragged it off, and buzzards finished the job.

"You believe in spirits, Pa?" Brady asked.

"Sometimes," Carter said as J. T. leaned a weary head on his father's shoulder. "You learn after a time that there's just no explanation for everything that happens. Got to be more than just earth and sky, today and tomorrow and last week. Who put the moon in the night sky? Wasn't old Walt here."

"He's old enough to've done it," J. T. remarked, then scrambled away before Walt's boot could reward the comment.

"Ma'd say it was God did all that," Brady argued. "Says so in the Book. Reverend Hollings reads it out on Sundays."

"Comanches would call it the great mystery," Carter explained. "All in all, it's just different words for the same thing."

"Reverend Hollings wouldn't say so," Brady declared. "He says the Indians are heathens and ought to be sent to the reservations where they can't hurt anybody."

"And what do you say?" Carter asked.

"I don't know," Brady admitted.

"J. T.?"

"I think what the reverend reads makes pretty good sense," the younger boy answered. "Ma sets great store by it, too, and she's not wrong too often. But for myself, I like Uncle Johnny's stories and his talk of sneaky coyotes and warriors walking on clouds. Sure is more fun racing ponies than doing lessons."

Walt laughed, and even Carter grinned a bit. He then directed the boys to bring in the rest of the wood.

"Those two are the best pieces of work you ever put your hand to, Carter Ross," old Walt pointed out when the boys had left. "You do as fine a job with the younger ones, and there'll be Rosses growing tall in these hills so long as there's water in the Brazos."

"It's mostly their ma's handiwork," Carter said. "And Johnny's, and yours. They'll have no easy time growing tall here, Walt. There are no bears to hunt, no buffalo running across the plains. Maybe no Johnny to spin tales and race ponies."

"I'd not give up on him just yet, son. Nighthawk's a man to make his way through hard times, and Johnny, why he's naught but a shadow, a bit of wind and sunshine that's here one minute and gone the next. No soldier boy'll bring him to that reservation."

Carter wondered. And as the snows of November continued into December, he worried more.

Hope, meanwhile, did her best to cheer him. In the evenings, Carter sat by the fireplace and listened as J. T. played a tune on his harmonica. Brady, Nathan, and Richmond would sing along. Sometimes even Rachel would pipe in a sweet note or two. Such times brought them all close, and the closeness drove off the despair of midwinter.

Two weeks short of Christmas, Hope collected the children in the back of a wagon and drove them into Palo Pinto. She kept her purpose a great mystery, and Carter pestered her for days afterward. There was a great amount of Bible reading and sewing going on, but he couldn't fathom the purpose of it.

"I never bother you with the details of a horse sale," Hope remarked when he asked why she purchased a bolt of white cloth. "Leave the house to my hands, Carter Ross!"

"I've seen such doings before," he told her. "There's a plot afoot, and it's bound sooner or later to hogtie me into doing something against my inclination. Probably against any hint of good judgment, too."

Still she kept her own counsel. Attempts to worm the truth out of Rachel or the boys failed miserably. Even stick candy bribes failed.

She's put the fear of God in 'em, Carter told himself when J. T. reluctantly turned down a peppermint stick. John Tyler Ross would kill for a bit of sugar under ordinary circumstances.

Three days before Christmas Hope greeted him at breakfast with an invitation to the church Christmas pageant in Palo Pinto.

"You know I don't give a hoot for that preacher," Carter told her. "That time when I took you to Sunday meeting, he talked till half the town was asleep. My back ached for a month, and my leg was so stiff I could barely walk you to the wagon. You'll never get me inside that jailhouse of a church again."

"It won't be at the church. We'll do it at the Snyders' barn. There's no preaching this time, either," Hope explained. "Besides, your children are in it."

"Eh?"

"It's what we've been doing in town," Nathan said, grinning like a raccoon that had just gorged himself in a henhouse. "We fooled you, didn't we? You never thought we could keep such a secret, I'll bet."

"You'd win," Carter said. "Brady, J. T.? You in this play?"

"We're shepherds," J. T. said without much enthusiasm. "Pa, we got tricked into it. Sort of."

"Oh?" Hope asked. "As I remember, you volunteered."

"That was because Lucy Crandall asked us to," Brady explained. "She's playing the angel."

"She'll make a good one, all right," Carter said, trying to keep a smile from bursting upon his lips. The way to get boys in Palo Pinto to do anything was to enlist Lucy's support.

"I'm a cherub," Rachel announced.

"Nate?" Carter asked as he drew Rachel up onto one knee.

"Rich and I get to sit in the loft and make this big star move," Nathan explained.

"We make animal noises, too," Richmond added. "I can moo pretty good. Reverend Hollings says I have to work on my donkey sound, though."

Carter couldn't help laughing, and as the youngsters explained their preparations, he knew Hope had woven her web expertly. Rachel even modeled her costume.

"I don't suppose I've got much choice," Carter said, surrendering. "Couldn't very well leave this little cherub to get to town on her own."

And so for the first time in months Carter Ross hauled his family into Palo Pinto. Stunned neighbors waved. Some dropped their jaws when they took note of the fact that there were no vegetables in the back ready for sale, that Carter brought no horses to barter or firewood to sell.

"Next thing you know Jasper Farrell will come to town ridin' his fat old sow," Ben Copeland declared.

"Lord must be smilin' to see such a sinner in church," Willa Snyder remarked. "Come along in, Carter. Meet your neighbors."

Carter first saw the children off the wagon and along to the stacked hay bales that served as a stage. He then escorted Hope inside.

"Good to see you, friend," Reverend Hollings said, gripping Carter's hand. "I don't think we could have presented this pageant if Hope hadn't gotten us organized."

The other ladies clapped, and Hope curtsied. She then set off to help Mrs. Hollings get the children in their places. Carter found himself sharing a corner of the barn with Ben Copeland.

"Heard from that brother of yours?" Copeland asked. "He out on the plains this winter, or has he dragged himself in with the rest of those Comanches?"

Carter gazed across the crowded barn at Hope. She was

tying a cravat knot for one of the Ludwell boys. Carter bit his lip and turned aside.

"You know, a man has a right to know if his neighbor takes scalps," Copeland went on. "Me, I'd as soon kill every red-skinned son of Satan in all of Texas. How do you feel about that, Ross?"

Carter walked away, but Copeland followed.

"You one of them Red Hearts, Ross?" the rancher asked. "Farrell told us how you fed those Kiowas. As I remember, the last time the Comanches rode through here, they left your stock be. I lost twenty horses, a whole summer's work. My best hand, Hank Jones, took an arrow through the knee."

"I've told you before," Carter said, halting his retreat and squaring his shoulders. "I'm sorry Henry got hurt. I'm sorry the horses were taken. I also told you it was none of my doing, Copeland, and I've grown tired of you hinting it was."

"We know who our friends are in this town," Copeland growled.

"Good. I never claimed to be any friend of yours," Carter replied, his face growing redder. "I'll trouble you to make no slurs against my name, else you'll find there's a consider-able difference between not being a man's friend and finding yourself his enemy."

"I suppose you'll have your redskin brother burn us out, huh?"

Carter balled his fist and would have slammed it into Copeland's face had not Hope's voice drawn his attention.

"Carter!" she called.

He glared furiously at Copeland, then wove his way through the crowd to where Hope struggled to separate a tangle of white-robed shepherds. Straw and boy and costume intertwined, and even Carter had a fight of it sorting the one from the other.

"Brady?" Carter cried in surprise as he pulled his eldest out of the pile. "J. T.?"

"Pa, he said something he shouldn't've," Brady explained.

"I can't repeat it just now, but he was talking about Uncle Johnny."

"I'll repeat it," J. T. offered. "It's a pretty fair word for a Porterfield!"

Silas Porterfield had three years and sixty pounds on J. T., but the raw-boned brawler shrank from the young boy's fiery eyes.

"Now what's this all about?" Carter asked. "J. T.?"

"He called Ma a squaw," J. T. answered. "Said something else, too, how she kept company with Indians while you were away to the war."

It was Carter's turn to scowl now, and Silas sought the shelter of a hay bale. A pair of smaller boys who'd gotten caught in the middle of things retreated hastily.

"I was just repeatin' what my pa said," Si pleaded. "Honest, Mr. Ross. Wasn't anything personal."

"There's not much of anything more personal," Carter said angrily. "You might keep in mind from now on, Si, that once you speak something, it's your words. You might have been able to use a friend on down the road, and you've like as not lost a couple this night."

J. T. nodded, and Brady angrily removed his robe and flung it at the makeshift stage.

"You should've let us finish it," Brady declared. "I'd whipped that Si black and blue."

"Not the time for that," Carter said, picking up the robe and leading the boys aside. "I know it's hard to leave words like that unanswered, but you won't get very far in this life hitting everybody who's got a cross word for you."

"Pa!" J. T. howled. "You should've heard the all of it."

"Doesn't matter," Carter said as Hope returned and began calming the others. "They should've kept their thoughts to themselves, and you should've stepped away. This play's important to your ma, and that's what really ought to be on your mind."

"You don't mean to say I have to put that thing back on

and play a shepherd?" Brady asked. "Pa, I'm like as not to pop that Si Porterfield right in the nose!"

"Not tonight," Carter said, slipping the robe over Brady's slender shoulders. "You know, one of the things my pa was most proud of was that no Ross ever started a job and left it hanging there. I've done my best to see it's stayed that way. Finish up, boys. As for those others, don't pay 'em much mind. It's your ma you should worry after."

"Yes, sir," the boys said in unison.

"Now take a deep breath and get along with the task at hand. It's a lot harder'n chopping firewood."

"Sure is," Brady agreed. Carter gave them a nudge toward the stage, and they brightened a bit.

"What set off the powderkeg?" Hope asked once the pageant began.

"Seems young Porterfield was less than cautious with his remarks," Carter explained. "Called their ma's character into question."

"What?"

"It appears I'm not the only one around to defend your honor, Hope. I believe they had Si fearing for his hide."

"Boys," she grumbled. "If the others could get a little better acquainted with Brady and J. T., there'd be less chance for this sort of misunderstanding."

"We've spoken on this before," Carter said, frowning. "I won't have them in that schoolhouse, listening to Reverend Hollings and his nonsense notions of the world. They're needed to help with the work, and besides, we aren't like other folks."

"And we won't be so long as you hide us behind that fence, Carter. Brady and J. T. have to learn to live in this world."

"They'll learn," Carter muttered. "I'll teach 'em."

"You don't know yourself," she complained.

Then they watched the pageant in silence. The shepherds proved a strange sight that night. Two in particular frowned heavily, and a third kept cautiously clear of the first two.

Only the three or four smaller ones seemed to follow the play. Lucy Crandall, as the angel, had to say "hark" three times before Brady responded.

Nevertheless, Nate and Rich worked the star perfectly, and little Rachel stole the show with her three lines. Carter praised them all, even J. T. and Brady, on the long ride homeward. J. T. gave a mock bow, and even Brady managed a grin. But once back home, all that changed. As the boys helped Carter unhitch the team from the wagon, J. T. leaned against his father and frowned.

"Hadley Copeland says we're Indians," J. T. said. "Are we, Pa?"

"Look at yourself, John Tyler Ross," Carter said, laughing. "Ever see a Comanche with hair as white as snow?"

"My hair's dark, like Uncle Johnny's," Brady said. "I don't know it all, Pa, but folks in town say our Grandma was a Comanche. I guess you took after your pa, just like J. T. Uncle Johnny took after your ma."

"After *his* ma," Carter explained. "It's a long story, and it's late, boys."

"I got to know," Brady said. J. T. nodded his agreement.

"I guess it's time then. Gather around. You won't find this like one of Johnny's tall tales, though. There's more sadness than I'd have you know."

"Tell us," Brady pleaded.

"All right," Carter said, swallowing. "To begin with, my mother was blond as summer wheat, golden yellow–haired with the brightest, bluest eyes you'll ever dream of. She was thin-faced like little Rachel, delicate as a garden flower. When we came to Texas, she wilted from the heat and never really got her health back. She died when I was very little.

"My father was in the army. I've told you that."

"Yes, sir," J. T. said. "Old Walt tells us all about his fighting in the Mexican War and all."

"It was just after he got back from Mexico that he met Swallow," Carter continued. "She was Johnny's ma, and as pretty and gentle a woman as I've ever known. I was, as I said, terribly little, and I'd been staying with some friends of Pa's in San Antonio. Swallow took me to her side, made me clothes, put meat on my bones and grit in my hide."

"She was an Indian?" Brady asked. "Your stepmother?"

"Comanche, daughter of Wolf That Runs. We had some good years. Johnny was born, and we crisscrossed Texas. Pa was posted at Ft. Mason for a time. Later we were up at old Ft. Belknap. Swallow didn't much like the forts, and the soldiers didn't take to her. So Pa bought some land here. He died before he had much of a chance to build anything. Old Walt, being Pa's oldest friend, took us in hand, but Swallow talked him into bringing us to Nighthawk, her brother. From then till I was grown, I was in Comanche camps most every summer. Winters we spent with Walt up in his cabin."

"So we're not Indians then," J. T. mumbled.

"No, not in the sense that we're blood kin anyway," Carter said. "But I'll admit my heart is often with 'em, and my own brother rides with Nighthawk still."

"Pa, they say all the Comanches have gone to the reservation," Brady said sadly. "You figure Uncle Johnny's there? Hadley says the ones that won't give themselves up are sure to freeze or starve."

"Some maybe," Carter admitted. "But Nighthawk knows the country, and he's got a rare talent for finding game. Johnny's been in tough spots before. I wouldn't bury him just yet."

"We won't," J. T. promised.

Carter pulled them close and wrapped an arm around their shoulders for a minute. Then he stepped back and sent the boys back to the task of unhitching the team.

No, he told himself, we won't bury Johnny for a long time to come.

CHAPTER 4

CHRISTMAS at the Ross home had always been a time of gathering family. That hard winter of '74, Carter drew Hope and the children close, somehow hoping their strength might stave off the pain that crept in from the world beyond Ross's Gap. As they collected around the fire with old Walt on Christmas Eve, singing songs and sharing recollections, Carter felt more than ever the absence of his brother.

Hope read it in his eyes, and when the children were finally chased to their beds and Walt departed for his cabin, she sat with Carter near the fire. They watched the flames dance along the charred remnants of oak and juniper logs, scarlets mixing with yellow and the occasional sweet blue glitter as juniper berries ignited and filled the air with their wintery scent.

"It's wrong to brood," she whispered. "I know you're upset about what happened at the pageant, and you're worried about Johnny, but you can't let that shut out all the good that's come to us."

Carter nodded and drew her to his side. But even the warmth of the fire and her tender touch couldn't entirely remove the sense of impending trial.

The arrival of the new year, 1875, did nothing to alleviate Carter Ross's fears. For a time the sun appeared, high and bright, sweeping with an invisible hand the glimmering sea of white from the landscape of Palo Pinto County. Then the gray veil returned, and an icy wind whined through the hills. Except for taking Brady and J. T. hunting in the rugged hills to the south, Carter kept close to home. Hailstones and sleet tormented the animals and made straying any great distance too great a risk.

Sometimes stagecoaches or farriers brought word of starving Comanches and Kiowas wandering across the plains, begging food or raiding ranches. Others staggered into Ft. Sill, defeated by weather and time. But there was no word of Quannah or the Kwahadis.

When the weather improved, Hope made a renewed effort to convince Carter to send the boys to school in town.

"If you have to take 'em into the church on Sundays, so be it," he grumbled. "But as to school, we've more books here than they've got in school, and I'd wager you're a better teacher than that preacher or his wife. You write a better hand, and you have the patience to tolerate a mistake by and by."

She begrudgingly accepted his withdrawal even though Carter knew the other women talked of their heathen neighbor, Carter Ross.

"Heathen?" he once cried out to Agnes Slocum. "My mother's father was baptizing Carolina farmers before most of you were walking. I'd read the Bible through by the time I was fifteen, and I never found mention of sermonizing half the day or judging your neighbors."

Hope had scowled.

"It's true," he declared later as he helped her hang up the week's washing.

"Maybe so," she told him, "but nobody likes having their words thrown back into their faces. Agnes and others are good people, and if you'd give them a chance to know you, they'd make fair friends."

"I don't need those kind of friends," Carter remarked. "I know 'em, Hope. They use you, borrow your talents, enlist your help, and in the end they cast you off like some worn-out plow. I agreed to ride to the war, didn't I? I served twice the time any man in this valley put in. Who among 'em looked in on you or the boys? Was Johnny saw to your needs, he and old Walt."

"That was a good ten years ago," she reminded him. "People had their own worries. Most of the families hereabouts weren't even here back then."

"Well, a man does best to keep to what he knows," Carter told her. "You do as you think best, Hope, but I know the hearts of these folks. They've never had any use for me, and deep down they resent Pa and Walt settling such a good piece of land and making peace instead of shooting Comanches."

Hope sighed and pinned a shirt to the clothesline. There was no arguing Carter into doing something he was dead set against. Her eyes betrayed that thought, and Carter judged she might have stronger words she wouldn't share.

For herself, Hope tried every way she knew to build a bridge to the neighbors. She helped with barn dances, visited the sick, even joined a Monday morning sewing circle. When she returned early the second week of the sewing circle meetings, he noticed her eyes red from crying.

"What's happened?" he asked.

"Nothing," she muttered.

"Hope? You won't convince me all's well, not with your eyes red as a tomato."

"Was Sarah Howard," she explained. "We met at her farm this time. I don't think I've ever shared three words with her in all the time she's lived down on Eagle Creek."

"You had words?"

"Oh, I didn't say anything," she barked, tossing her sewing aside. "She did all the talking, and I just raced off like a beaten dog."

"What'd she say?" Carter asked, drawing Hope to him. "Tell me."

"She said she wouldn't have savages under her roof," Hope said, shuddering with anger. "She said her boy Charles was scalped by Comanches in '64, and she knew full well there were those about who had a hand in it."

"Meaning me," Carter growled. "She's got a short memory. I was off fighting Yanks in '64. Fact is, I toted her oldest, Jefferson, from half a regiment of Yank infantry that summer when his horse went down."

"She wasn't talking about you," Hope went on. "She meant me. She said I was harboring Indians, feeding and clothing the very ones that killed her boy."

"I'll settle this," Carter said, slipping away from her and angrily storming toward the corral. "She had no call to . . ."

"Carter, please," Hope called. "She was hurt, and she knew Johnny was here."

"That's right. He was here looking after my family. He wasn't riding with Nighthawk. I never knew either of 'em to make war on children anyway. Charlie was what, eleven? I put shoes on his first pony when he was Nate's age. I cried when I heard from Jeff what happened. To think Johnny'd had a hand in it! Eleven years old and nigh as tall as a fencepost. About as old as those dead Kiowa boys Captain Kendall was taking to Ft. Sill. I wonder how many of the little ones in those wagons died since first snow. Suppose Sarah Howard'll shed tears for any of 'em?"

"They'll never look at things your way, Carter. You see those Indians as friends, as people deserving your compassion. Most people here view the Comanches and Kiowas as a nuisance, human coyotes to be shot or driven off."

"I know," he said sadly. "And it's why I leave them to their own ways and keep to mine."

She nodded, then gripped his hand and led the way inside. Reverend Hollings appeared later to speak of forgiveness and understanding, and Hope returned next week to the sewing circle. There was no apology from Sarah Howard, no word of sympathy or compassion from the other ladies.

"You've got a forgiving nature, Hope," Carter told her. "Me, I'd told the whole bunch to go to blazes."

As February approached, Carter occupied himself driving a dozen horses to market in Weatherford. He also supplied seven remounts to the cavalry at Ft. Griffin. He spoke to the soldiers at the fort, and he shared a winter's camp with other horse traders west of Weatherford. But he had only hard stares and silence for the hard-hearted neighbors who had brought Hope to tears.

The first night of February a storm blew in from the west, rattling shutters and sending icy splinters of wind through cracks in the plank walls of the house. The young boys and Rachel huddled with their mother beside the fireplace. Carter kept J. T. and Brady busy tending the stock in the barn. Wolves howled at the cloud-draped moon, and an uneasiness settled over the land.

"Fetch my rifle, Brady," Carter ordered when the horses back at the corral reared and whinnied. "We've got company."

Brady dashed out the side door of the barn, and Carter motioned J. T. into the safety of the tack room. Soon Brady returned with a seldom-used Winchester repeater and a box of shells. Carter hurriedly loaded the rifle's magazine, then escorted both boys back to the house before setting off toward the corral.

With the moon hidden from view, darkness engulfed the barnyard. Squawking chickens and anxious horses directed Carter Ross's movements. He moved slowly, silently, his shadowy figure blending into the night. When he reached the corral, he detected three shivering figures trying to throw short ropes over the heads of the nervous horses.

"Hold it right there, boys," Carter bellowed as he cocked the rifle. The warning or the none-too-subtle click of the cocked hammer stilled the three shadows. The smallest turned slowly and stretched his hands to his sides. He stepped closer, and Carter frowned in recognition. Before him, bare but for the frayed remnant of an old trade blanket, stood Owl Eyes, Nighthawk's youngest boy.

"I never knew a Kwahadi to steal an unbroken horse when

there's a barn full of good saddle mounts twenty yards away," Carter grumbled.

"I'm not such a good thief as some I know," the boy said, motioning his brothers along. The other boys were uneasy, and Carter turned the rifle aside.

"Runs Long, Buffalo Hump," he spoke. "How is your father?"

The boys stared at Carter with hollow eyes. Runs Long, at fifteen, should have been playing a flute in the winter lodge of some maiden. Buffalo Hump, thirteen, stumbled along, his eyes full of hunger and confusion. Neither boy was clothed any better than his younger brother.

"Come along to the house," Carter said, waving them along. "Sit by my fire and tell me what brought you here."

"Horses," a deeper voice called from the darkness.

Carter instinctively turned in that direction, and the young Comanches fled.

"Boys, come back!" Carter called.

"Come!" the other voice beckoned, and the boys halted their flight. Moments later they followed a tall, dark-eyed Indian toward Carter.

"Nighthawk," Carter said, gripping the Comanche's wrist firmly. "Old friend."

"I'm glad you still call me that," Nighthawk said, smiling warily. "It's not so good a time for the Kwahadi."

"Nor for any of us," Carter said, leading them toward the house. "But hard times don't change a man's heart."

"No," Nighthawk agreed, resting a hand on Carter's shoulder as they walked. "I'm sorry I didn't trust you. No blood flows between us, and we haven't been welcome elsewhere."

"There are other bonds than those forged of blood," Carter said, swallowing deeply as they approached the door. "But blood bonds are deep. What do you know of Johnny?"

The door then swung open, and J. T. stepped outside. At his side stood Johnny Ross, wrapped in one of Hope's quilts and grinning with exhausted eyes.

"You'll never be the thief your cousin is," Carter remarked to the boys. "He could steal a man's pants in midwinter."

"Soon I'll have to," Johnny said, wrapping the quilt around Nighthawk as the weary warrior led the way inside. Carter felt his heart sigh as he looked at the ribs protruding through Johnny's bronze flesh, at hips narrowed by the ravages of hunger and desperation.

The boys darted after their father, and J. T. directed them to the fire. Carter shut the door and followed. Only as the firelight illuminated the five visitors did their real plight become evident. Bare feet bloodied from the rocky trail and thighs torn by mesquite thorns and cactus spines spoke of the long, bitter escape from Palo Duro.

"Children, make room for your cousins," Hope said as she hurried to set a kettle on the coals. "I'll have some coffee ready, Johnny, and Brady's readying what's left of tonight's stew."

Johnny managed a nod and a grin in reply, then grasped his brother's hands.

"I wouldn't have come, but there was nowhere else to go," Johnny explained. "We thought to take horses, borrow supplies, then ride elsewhere. But your ears're still sharp, brother."

"Yes," Carter said, smiling. "Where would you go, though? This is your home. As for borrowing, when did I ever have anything that wasn't yours?"

The words brought sudden comfort, and Johnny joined the others at the fire. The warmth stopped the shivers, and shortly Hope passed out cups of bubbling coffee and plates of beef stew. Life returned to empty eyes.

"Brady, why don't you and J. T. clear out your room for your Uncle Johnny," Carter said. "Take some of those old mattress covers out to the barn and stuff 'em with hay. I don't suppose you'll mind sharing the front room with these cousins."

"Sure, Pa," J. T. said, nudging a more reluctant Brady along.

"There's no need," Johnny objected. "We'll sleep in the barn."

"It's too cold," Carter complained. "You'll want the fire tonight. Besides, these youngsters might decide to practice their thieving craft, and I could wake up without my best horses."

Owl Eyes turned and grinned. Carter bent down and squeezed the twelve-year-old's bony shoulder, and even Buffalo Hump seemed to relax. Soon Hope was doling out spare nightshirts. Brady and J. T. spread mattresses out on the floor, and all prepared to settle in for a peaceful night.

"I think you've forgotten to make some introductions," Hope whispered, pointing to the far corner of the room where Nathan huddled with Richmond and Rachel. Carter hurried over, lifted the three of them and carried the squirming, squawking children to the fire.

"This is your Uncle Johnny," Carter explained as he turned the three little ones over to the tall, dark-haired skeleton. "You remember the summer he came, and we rode out to Rock Creek, Nate."

"We caught catfish," the boy mumbled.

"Was your uncle carved the little wolves on your bedposts, Rich," Carter added. "Rachel, Johnny brought the rabbit hides your ma made into that pretty winter bonnet you like to wear."

A faint recollection came to the children's eyes, and Johnny matched it with a magical sparkle as he embraced each of the little ones in turn.

Nighthawk and his boys were strangers, and Nate in particular eyed them with suspicion. J. T. and Owl Eyes were quickly swapping tales, though, and that quieted any remaining fears. As the ground shook with thunder, and the wind whined through the trees, the children boasted and laughed and sang.

"Thank you for this gift of gladness," Nighthawk said as he stood with Carter and watched a fresh brightness invade eyes too often possessed by despair.

"Gifts should be returned in kind, and this one is a long time overdue," Carter explained. "Do you remember when old Walt rode into your camp with me and Johnny? We were as scruffy a pair as any orphans ever set loose on the plains. You took us in, gave us a home and a family."

"You came with my sister," Nighthawk explained. "Johnny was my blood, my son."

"I wasn't."

"Ah, but you had the wind in your feet," Nighthawk said, grinning as the memory swept over him. "Never had I seen a white boy who could fly across the land. And when you rode! The spirits must have given your heart to the horses."

"As I remember, I got thrown my share."

"The spirits remind us we're flesh sometimes. Or maybe they enjoy a funny sight."

"Maybe," Carter admitted. "Anyway, I'm glad you came."

"There was no other place but death," Nighthawk said sadly.

"So it was for me. I pray you'll grow strong here, that your sons will know the good life you showed me."

"That is all gone, my friend, dead with the thousand ponies. Even as the hawk feeds on its prey, death tears at my heart."

"It's a sad time," Carter agreed, "but nothing is certain. Times change like the summer wind. And perhaps better days lie ahead."

CHAPTER 5

YES, the world has a strange way of turning, Carter thought those next few days. It wasn't so long ago Nighthawk had knelt beside a younger Carter Ross, tending scraped knees and battered elbows that were part of Kwahadi boyhood. Now it was Carter's turn to tend the man that seemed as much an uncle as Swallow seemed a mother.

Hope actually did most of the labor. She had a gentle touch ministering to the tired, near-starved boys, and even Nighthawk was set at ease by her soft voice and gentle hands.

"You chose well," Nighthawk told Carter. "For a time I thought you crazy to take a white woman. They're too lazy. This one works like a Kwahadi—hard. She isn't scared to see blood, and she's pretty. It's well whites don't ask horses for their women. You would be poor, my friend."

Carter laughed and nodded his head. Hope, who heard most of it, flashed a mock frown and went on with her duties. Her nursing repaired torn feet and patched scratches. Her nourishing food restored spirits and returned strength. In a week's time J. T. and Brady were at a loss to hold their own against their wrestling guests. Even a fresh flurry of snowflakes couldn't dampen the boys' enthusiasm.

Johnny watched his cousins and nephews with interest. Often he'd draw them together at night and share stories. Sometimes Nighthawk would take a turn, and once Carter provided a tale. Eventually Hope brought little Rachel over, and though the Indians were a bit put off by the inclusion of females in what was obviously a council of warriors, they allowed it. After all, Hope had proven her worth as a medicine woman, and Rachel's smile was always welcome.

47

From time to time, usually after supper, J. T. would take out a guitar bartered off a cowboy and play some tune taught him by Put Daniels on a slow day at the way station over on Bluff Creek. Most times J. T. would have to substitute a word or two, as his mother was solidly opposed to swearing, but the music provided good cheer, and Carter was especially fond of listening to J. T.'s clear, sweet voice narrate one of Put's old ballads.

As the Comanche boys grew strong again, Brady and J. T. provided clothing. Johnny would take the whole bunch up the creek to shoot rabbits or stalk deer. Fresh meat was welcome, and hides were tacked to the barn for stretching. Later they would provide more appropriate garments for grumbling youngsters not at all accustomed to buttons or sleeves or trouser legs.

"For now it's best to wear the white man's clothes," Johnny advised. "They warm you against winter's chills, and they conceal you from your enemies. There is another thing, too."

Hope appeared with a pair of shears. As a further precaution, she prepared to clip her guests' hair. For several minutes there was a Comanche rebellion. Then Nighthawk clapped his hands and offered himself to the barber.

"Father?" Owl Eyes cried in disbelief. "We won't be Kwahadis anymore. Already we grow into Tonkawa lap dogs."

"You don't change a man's heart by cutting his hair," Nighthawk announced. "These are our friends. They run grave risks, as we do also. By the time the leaves come back to the white oaks, our hair will grow, and we will again ride the Llano. Now we must stay and rest, grow strong on the meat of the deer we will kill. To grow we must first stay alive."

Even clipped and wearing trousers and sheepskin coats, a Kwahadi Comanche's face didn't change. There was no concealing the proud nose, the sharp eyes, or the bronze skin. And so whenever riders approached, as they did more and more, Johnny would whistle, and the boys would vanish inside the house or barn, scamper down the creek, or melt into the trees.

Most of the time the horsemen were lost, bound for the stage station or searching for the best route into Palo Pinto. Twice, columns of soldiers used the gap through the hills to cross the Brazos at the wooden bridge on the Jacksboro market road. Then, toward the end of February, a different variety of visitor appeared—Jasper Farrell. With the scout were two young Tonkawa warriors and three farmers from upriver.

"Mind if we have a look around the place?" Farrell asked, motioning for the Indians to examine the horses in the corral.

"Looks like you plan to do it even if I do," Carter answered angrily. "You're not welcome on my land, Farrell."

"Oh, but I am," Farrell said, drawing papers from his pocket and waving them in the air. "I knew you would be the one to try and stop us, Ross. Well, I've got a military order to search this valley for signs of hostile Indians and a court order from Judge Bastrop allowin' me free run of the county."

"Then I guess you'll look us over. You figure there's a Comanche hiding in my henhouse? Maybe one's in the loft."

"We'll look, Ross. You count on it. Everybody hereabouts knows where your sympathies lie. You were raised with 'em. Maybe you're white on the outside, but we know what's underneath."

"I'd think you'd be content having run down all those Kiowas," Carter grumbled.

"You don't know the half of it," Farrell boasted. "We run across another batch just last week up along the Trinity not far from Buffalo Springs. Kids mostly, and near naked. No fight left in 'em, so Cap'n Kendall fed 'em, threw some blankets around 'em, and packed 'em north to Ft. Sill."

"You're a long way from Buffalo Springs now," Carter observed. "What brought you down here?"

"Comanches," Farrell said, reaching into his saddlebags and snatching a child's cornstalk doll. "Comanches, like that brother of yours. They've been helpin' themselves to some Young County livestock. We trailed 'em to the river. There's signs all over the place. I found this in one of their old camps. Shoot, the little girl that owned it wasn't a quarter mile away. Show him, Tom."

One of the farmers drew out a bundle of hair and waved it in the air. Farrell motioned toward Carter, and the man tossed it. Carter reached down and reverently lifted the scalp. Raven black and soft to the touch, he thought as he threw it at Farrell's face. So now they were murdering children!

"Told you he was soft-hearted where Indians were concerned," Farrell said, laughing as he returned the scalp to the farmer. "Tom, you and the Tonks search the barn. I'll have a look in the house."

"No, you won't," Hope declared, appearing in the door with a loaded shotgun.

"I've got the authority!" Farrell shouted, waving his papers at her.

"I know no law in *my* state that allows a foul-mouthed, evil-smelling braggart to invade *my* home," she responded. "You do what you want with those papers, but take a step toward *my* house, and I'll scatter you and those papers halfway to Kansas."

"Well, Jasper?" the farmer named Tom asked. "You goin' to let a woman put you off?"

"No," Farrell declared, pocketing his papers. "Find anything in the barn?"

The Tonkawas emerged shaking their heads, and Farrell motioned them toward their horses.

"What about the house?" Tom asked.

"You see any tracks lead this way?" Farrell asked the Indians. Both shook their heads, and Farrell turned back toward the river. "No need, Tom. Even a man loves Indians wouldn't have 'em to sit down to dinner in his very own house."

"You're just afraid of that woman," the second farmer declared.

"Not the woman, Rod," Farrell said, laughing loudly. "That scattergun."

The others laughed, too, and the riders galloped off to the north. Once they were out of sight, Johnny slipped past Hope and joined Carter.

"They will return," the younger man muttered. "We must be gone."

"It's too soon," Carter objected. "Wait for first thaw."

"Can't," Johnny said, nervously leading Carter aside. "That doll. Nighthawk made it for his granddaughter."

"What? You mean there are others nearby?"

"They were going to the reservation," Johnny explained. "We separated way back in what, November maybe. Nighthawk's girl, Brave Heart Woman, went with Dancing Bear."

"I guess they changed their mind."

"Or had it changed. This one, Farrell? His heart is dark with hatred."

"Raiders killed his brother Fitzhugh at Elm Creek."

"Yes, many died then," Johnny mumbled. "Kiowas still sing of that as the bad medicine raid. No bullets were stopped that time."

"That's how it will be if they catch you. Stay here. Nobody knows about the cellar. It's a safe place."

"Nighthawk will never stay now," Johnny said sadly. "Brave Heart Woman is his only daughter. His wife is dead. Also Swift Antelope and Two Bears, his brothers. We are all that are left."

"And if you ride out there, how long can you survive? Farrell's got as dark a heart as you think, and he's got sharp eyes. He and those Tonkawas will pick up your trail. Johnny, you're the only brother I'll ever have."

"There is too much danger," Johnny declared. "For you and for us. Better we should go."

"To Walt's place then," Carter reluctantly suggested. "I'll haul what supplies we can spare up there. You, Nighthawk, and the boys can follow by night."

"We need horses."

"There are seven or eight mustangs up in Walt's corral. We planned to take 'em to Weatherford first chance. They're shod, but I didn't brand 'em."

"One day I will pay you."

"You did that a hundred times over when you looked after Hope and the little ones while I was away. Johnny, I wish you'd reconsider. Those youngsters are just starting to get some color back. That Owl Eyes is still little more than a stick about the waist."

"He'll grow stronger. He's small, but like J. T. full of song and sound of heart."

Carter sighed, then turned toward the house. Hope stood as before, blocking the door with her shotgun.

"Don't tell me you're barring the door even to your own husband?" Carter asked.

"Got a warrant, mister?" she asked in turn.

"No, but I'll help the pretty outlaw pack some cornmeal."

She nodded, then set aside the shotgun and escorted him to the kitchen.

Carter had never been much good at farewells, and Johnny didn't believe in them. The two brothers loaded a wagon in silence. Then Johnny led Nighthawk and the boys into the cover of some nearby trees, and Carter drove the wagon along to Antelope Mountain where Walt's cabin awaited.

The Indians beat Carter there. Old Walt hobbled about the porch in rare humor, obviously glad of the company. By the time Carter and Johnny unloaded the supplies, Walt was spinning tales of bygone times.

"I'll bring Brady and J. T. up later in the week," Carter

promised as the last of the deer hides were carried inside the cabin.

"Don't," Johnny said, clasping his brother's wrists. "Soon we must leave, and that will be hard. I'll do it, brother, but with a heavy heart. You must let me take my own path, even if it's not one I take with a glad heart. You have to go your own way, too. We've always known that, you and me."

"Johnny, there's only death out on the plains."

"What is life but a long preparation for death? Kwahadis don't fear it, remember?"

I remember everything, Carter thought as he climbed atop the wagon. I recall the night I sat beside you and Swallow as fever raged through our camp. I can still hear your feverish prayers. I prayed, too, back then. I asked for Swallow to get well. I asked that peace come. Well, Swallow died, and war followed. That's what comes of prayer!

Carter tried to work the bitterness out of heart on the ride homeward. It just wasn't possible. Back at the house, Brady and J. T. had erased all traces of the visitors. Straw was returned to the barn, and mattress covers were folded and stowed away. It was as if Johnny had never come.

But he had.

Jasper Farrell seemed to know it, too. The scout returned often to search for tracks. The third time a dozen ranchers rode along.

"Seen your Comanche friends lately?" Farrell called. "They've been busy. Hit three or four ranches across the Brazos in two nights. I'd judge they ran off forty horses."

"I lost fifteen myself!" Ben Copeland shouted. "Farrell says you know where they are, Ross! Tell me!"

"Farrell's a fool if he says that," Carter declared. "What good would forty horses do me? I chase more ponies than I can handle out of these hills each spring. What's more, your animals are branded, aren't they? You think I'm a rustler, Copeland? You may not like me for a neighbor, but I never figured you for an idiot."

"I never claimed you took stock yourself," Farrell pointed out. "Only that you'd know where to find them that did."

"Sorry, folks, but I've had my own business to conduct."

"Let's have a look around," Copeland suggested, and the others voiced their approval. Copeland pointed toward the barn, and three riders dismounted and had a look. Others searched the animal sheds. Carter barred their entry to the house, though.

"Get out of the way!" a fat rancher named Hake ordered as he drew a pistol. Carter pulled his own and shot his assailant in the arm.

"Murder!" Hake cried. "He's killed me."

"Stuff a kerchief in the hole," Farrell shouted. "Quiet yourself."

"Not the house," Carter said as Farrell stepped toward the door.

"I'll do it myself, just take a quick glance or two," Farrell promised.

"You wouldn't stand for it yourself, Farrell," Carter said as Hope appeared, shotgun in hand. "Law's specific. You've got to know who or what you're looking for."

"Goin' to a lot of trouble to make us think you've got 'em in there, aren't you?" Farrell asked. "Well, I'd guess them well to the north. We'll try that way for a time. But we'll be back, Ross. Bank on that!"

CHAPTER 6

FEBRUARY's close brought more news of the elusive Comanche raiders. Twice, haggard ranchers rode up Ioni Creek with news that cattle or horses had vanished in the night. Two wagons were burned at the Lowell farm up in Young County, and the westbound stage was chased just north of the Brazos crossing.

Carter received the news grimly. The raids had the entire frontier nervous, and scouting parties from Ft. Griffin crossed the countryside often, occasionally rounding up a few derelict Comanches or Kiowas to be carted to Ft. Sill. Sometimes gunshots would mark the death of some defiant warrior. Carter cringed as he thought of Johnny, Nighthawk, or one of the boys caught in the open, mercilessly shot down. True, the soldiers generally tried to bring in prisoners, but Jasper Farrell and others delighted in shooting anyone that even half resembled a Comanche.

Carter tried to stay clear of Walt's place. Farrell kept someone watching the Ross ranch most days, and regular visits would certainly have encouraged Farrell to pay Walt and his guests a visit. But after the Howard farm was raided, angry bands of farmers and ranchers scoured the county. Carter set off to warn his brother.

First he led young Terry King, Farrell's spy, on a wild ride through the tangled briars and scrub trees south of the gap. Even Nighthawk would have had difficulty staying with Carter's elusive shadow, and the King boy was soon ensnarled in thorns and left hopelessly behind. Carter continued to Walt's place to pass on his news.

The cabin appeared abandoned, but as Carter came closer,

55

a whistle identified him as friend. Buffalo Hump and Owl Eyes popped out of the trees and finished chopping kindling. Old Walt stepped out from the cabin's narrow doorway. Johnny led Runs Long out of the barn. Only Nighthawk failed to appear.

"I don't know it was any too wise you coming out here," Walt said as Carter climbed down from his mount. "Been a lot of riders by here of late."

"By my place as well," Carter replied. "Soldiers down at the river, too. I thought it best you should know."

"We know," Johnny announced.

"Did you also know there've been raids on the neighboring farms?" Carter asked. "People are pretty stirred up. It's best you keep to cover."

"Maybe so," Johnny said as he motioned Carter off toward the barn. "But the time for hiding is over."

Carter thought to reply, but as Johnny motioned for Runs Long to join his brothers near the woodpile, Carter swallowed his words. There was something unspoken, a darkness crossing Johnny's brow. And as they continued past the barn and out onto the mountainside, Carter kept silent.

Once they were clear of the cabin and barn, Antelope Mountain came to life. Squirrels bounded from tree to tree. Lizards darted between rocks. A deer appeared in the brush, and a crow cried out at the human intruders below.

Carter and Johnny were not the only ones on the mountain, though. A group of slender figures dressed in deerskins threaded their way through the trees twenty yards away. Carter scowled as he read the brands stamped onto the rumps of their horses. The Diamond C of Ben Copeland, the Farrell brothers' FB, and the Lazy H Howard brand were all represented. Three cavalry mounts appeared as well.

"Johnny?" Carter cried. "You knew they were here?"

"I'm their brother, as you are mine," Johnny explained. "Where else should they come?"

"But . . ."

"Come," Johnny said, taking his older brother's arm and leading him along. "This isn't the day to argue."

Johnny wove his way up the mountain along a rocky path etched recently by dragging logs. A hundred yards ahead, the path climbed alongside a chalk cliff torn from the mountain by some ancient rock slide. There was an eerie feeling to the place, and Carter paused more than once to shake off a sense of dread. Johnny, too, hesitated before continuing along to the top. There, a ledge offered a tremendous view of the Brazos and its countless tributary creeks, which cut the northeast quadrant of Palo Pinto County. But it wasn't the river or the hills beyond that unsettled Carter Ross.

At the far northern edge of the cliff stood three burial scaffolds. The nearest held a body covered with one of Hope's quilts. A splendid bow of white ash lay alongside the corpse.

"No," Carter mumbled, recalling how as a boy of fourteen he'd used that bow to fell a buck in the hills a half mile away. Its owner had been the gentle guiding hand, the tolerant voice, the heroic warrior, and true friend who had taken the place of a dead father.

"It's a good place," Johnny whispered as he sat on a nearby rock and dropped his chin into his hands. "Nighthawk was fond of high places."

Johnny then sang softly an ancient tune, a mourning hymn of sorts. Carter joined in, though the words were only a faint memory now. He hadn't had the chance to sing for Swallow, though. Now he felt he had to mourn her fallen brother.

"How did it happen?" Carter asked, shuddering as the terrible realization tore through him.

"Two boys came to the cabin," Johnny explained. "They came seeking food. It was late, and Nighthawk thought only of the hunger. He left with Runs Long. When they reached the river, men came from nowhere, riding and shooting. It was over quickly, and he knew no pain. Only Runs Long escaped to the trees."

"He was a good man."

"He was our father," Johnny said angrily. "We shared his lodge and his fire. I'll find these men."

"You'll only get yourself killed," Carter objected. "Please, Johnny, can't you see? It's all over. There's no place to hide, no refuge to be found."

"We'll go west, to the Llano. Soon it'll be summer. We'll find the buffalo."

"They're all gone. You'll find only death."

"Then I pray it will come as quickly for me," Johnny said, turning toward the scaffolds.

They remained together for half an hour, sharing the silence and remembering other times. Then Johnny led the way back to Walt's cabin. When they arrived, Johnny found a small band of Comanches assembled. None appeared any older than Runs Long. He and Owl Eyes were tying bundles onto ponies' backs. Buffalo Hump readied a pale mustang.

"No," Carter pleaded, holding Johnny's arm. Only now did the recent scratches of mesquite thorns draw Carter's attention.

"You see," Johnny said sadly. "It's too late. Blood will have blood. We must leave now."

"There's another choice," Carter argued. "You could come back with me to the ranch. You have as much right to the place as I do. You could stay there."

"They couldn't," Johnny said, pointing to Nighthawk's three sons. "I, too, miss the old days, Cart, but they're gone. As Nighthawk was a father to me, now I must be a father to them. Remember me to my other sons."

Carter gripped his brother's hands. Johnny's fingers had grown cold as if the icy breath of death was already upon him.

"One day soon we'll again hunt the buffalo together," Johnny whispered as he started toward the waiting pony. "One day soon."

Carter doubted it. The air had grown cold, and a shrill

wind whined across the mountain. Off in the distance an owl cried. For such a creature of the night to call out in the early afternoon was an ill omen indeed.

Carter remained at the cabin as the Comanches melted into the far horizon. Old Walt spoke of half-forgotten times, of old ghosts and often-told tales. Toward dusk Carter headed homeward, his heart heavy with a great sadness.

"Lord, keep him safe," Carter prayed for the first time in ages. "Hold him close. Protect him." But few of Carter's prayers had ever been answered, and he tried to cast from his mind the sight of another scaffold on that far mountainside.

Three days later, Jasper Farrell led a youthful-looking lieutenant and a dozen blue-shirted cavalrymen across Ioni Creek. Carter met them, shotgun in hand, as they approached the house.

"Anybody didn't know better'd think you weren't glad to see me," Farrell called out.

"About as glad to see you as a winter blizzard," Carter replied. "What do you want, Farrell?"

"Brought news," the scout explained. "We've been sweepin' the countryside of your friends. Just the other day we happened upon a band of Comanches. Bucks gave us a bit of a time, but the women and kids came in peaceful enough afterward."

Carter's answer was a cold stare, but Farrell only laughed.

"Kiowas are finished," Farrell went on to say. "Lone Wolf himself stumbled into Ft. Sill. Wasn't anything left for 'em to eat but their moccasins. Already ate all the dogs and horses."

"So what's that got to do with me?" Carter asked.

"Thought you'd want to pass on the news to your friends," Farrell answered. "Those that don't turn themselves in are in for a hard time of it, you know."

Carter wondered if there could be a harder time for the Comanches than had already befallen them. Probably not.

"Do you have any business with me, Lieutenant?" Carter finally asked the young officer in charge.

"Mr. Farrell seemed to think you might know where to find some renegade Comanches," the lieutenant replied.

"I don't think Farrell thinks much at all," Carter declared. "As to Comanches, I know nothing."

"Thought as much," the lieutenant grumbled. "Come along, Farrell. It's a long ride back to the fort. Appears to me this whole trip's been wasted."

Farrell glanced angrily at Carter, then followed the soldiers as the column turned westward.

For better than a week, an uneasy peace settled over Ross's Gap. No cavalry patrols crossed the Brazos, and no raiding Comanches appeared at neighboring ranches. Unfortunately, the peace was fleeting, and once again Jasper Farrell led a band of riders across Ioni Creek.

There were no soldiers this time, and Carter noted the fact with no small satisfaction.

"Hold on there!" Carter shouted, displaying his shotgun. "You've got no cavalry squad behind you this time, and I see no badge. You've no right on my land, and you're not welcome here!"

"Didn't expect you'd receive me with a parade," Farrell responded, turning to his six companions. "Told you, friends."

"What do you want?" Carter asked impatiently.

"Brought some news," Farrell answered. "And an offer. I'm not ridin' with the cavalry anymore. That's true enough. 'Course, they never did pay worth a fiddle, and I can't abide those fuzzy-cheeked lieutenants."

"Get on with it, Farrell," Dick Loring urged. "Tell him."

"All right," Farrell agreed. "We've had some trouble down-river. The Copeland place got hit hard. Morgan Hart was shot, and young Jim Latham was hatcheted in the arm. Two dozen cows got run off, and some horses were taken. We trailed 'em to the river, but they were clever and hid their trail well."

"That's hard news," Carter said, gazing at his feet. Hart was a good man with a rope, and Latham had once worked at the stage station over on the Jowell ranch.

"Were only ten or so of 'em," Loring added. "Mostly young, some no older'n Hadley and little Moss. Their leader was a tall fellow with blazing eyes. He painted himself with white paint and rode a pale mustang. I swear I shot him myself three or four times, but you'd never know it. Ben calls him the gray ghost."

"Tell me, Ross, what manner of man rides a white horse and paints his face white, then goes raidin' by the dark of night?" Farrell asked.

"A man with strong medicine," Carter said uneasily. Or one that doesn't care whether he lives or dies, he thought.

"More likely somebody unsure of his men," Loring suggested. "He's out to prove himself unkillable. Well, that's not possible. You remember that Kiowa back in '64 rode down on us, got a bullet for his trouble? Well, we'll get this Gray Ghost the same way."

"Not without help," Farrell grumbled. "Listen, Ross, I know you've got old ties to the Comanches, but these savages killed some neighbors of yours. They could come to your place next. Come with us. You know this country, and you know the Comanches. Show us where they're at. We'll do the rest."

"Ben's offered a thousand-dollar reward for the ghost," Loring added. "You'd receive a share. You can't tell me some cash money wouldn't be welcome, either. Times are hard."

"I don't have the time," Carter told them.

"Wouldn't take long," Farrell argued. "There'd be those who took note of your help."

"I did my fighting back in Tennessee," Carter explained. "I have no stomach for killing nowadays, and I've no heart for murdering Indians."

"Just for seein' 'em murder white folks, eh?" Loring accused. "You were right, Farrell."

"You'll be sorry you turned us down," Farrell promised. "Wait and see."

Carter wasn't swayed by threats, though. He waved his shotgun at them, and Farrell led the way back toward Ioni Creek.

Jasper Farrell did his best to make good on the promise. He rode along the river and spread word of Carter's refusal. Whenever Hope or the boys were in town, angry accusations met their ears. Some stores and shops denied them service, and once J. T. returned from a trip to the way station bleeding from a swollen mouth.

"It's all right, Pa," the boy said. "There were three of 'em, and the whole bunch is like to be sorry they tangled with me."

The sight of J. T.'s swollen lip, of a sour-faced Brady, and a solemn Hope stirred a decade of resentment inside Carter. He hated Farrell and the others for bringing such sorrow on the innocent. And he worried that he might not be able to avoid the storm swirling over Palo Pinto County.

"I feel like I'm sitting on the point of a lance, trying hard to hold on," Carter told old Walt Harper. "They want me to ride out after my own brother, and I can't do it."

"It's a hard time," Walt said, nodding. "It's not easy to know what's the right thing to do. It's harder on Johnny, though. His heart will sour with killing. There'll be no place to run to."

"No," Carter agreed. "No refuge for any of us."

That very night gunshots echoed down the river. Little Richmond howled in fear, and J. T. had Carter's shotgun loaded and waiting by the time Carter pulled on a pair of trousers and raced to the door. An uneasy silence followed. Then shadowy riders arrived.

"Hold there!" Carter yelled, taking aim on the closest figure. "Who's there?"

"Jasper Farrell!" Farrell called out. "Been chasin' Comanches."

"There are no Comanches here," Carter replied calmly. He'd regained his composure, and as the moon darted out of the clouds, he could read the anxious faces of neighbors gathering alongside Farrell.

"I come to make you the same offer as last time," Farrell explained. "What's more, we whittled 'em down some. They're on the run, and it ought not to be much trouble ridin' 'em down."

"Be good sport," Dick Loring boasted.

"We could use a man can speak with 'em," Ben Copeland added. "I'd pay you for your time."

"I won't take money for hunting men," Carter objected. "I mind my own affairs and leave others to do the same."

"This should be your affair," Copeland replied angrily. "They shot up my house, scared my family to distraction. They could hit your place next."

"Not likely," one of the darkened figures in back grumbled.

"Indian lovers, the whole bunch of 'em," another piped in.

"We'll remember your refusin'," Farrell said. "Come on, Ross. Let's have done with it once and for all. Look, we'll do the rest just like these two."

Loring led forward a pair of ponies. Slung across the horses were a pair of bare, lifeless bundles. Farrell made a motion with his hand, and Loring cut the bodies loose. Both fell to the ground, and their ponies bolted.

Carter turned away. He shuddered as he envisioned Johnny's lifeless eyes, the familiar brightness gone forever. He wanted to run away, hide from the awful sight. He didn't. Slowly he cracked his eyes open.

Death often proved a great trickster. Rather than grant the peace the old so often welcomed, she struck out at the young, the innocent, the inexperienced. As Carter stared at the lifeless faces, he cried inside. The first Indian was maybe nineteen. His chest was torn by five bullets. A sixth pierced his forehead. One finger was missing, likely cut to free a ring. He was also scalped.

The second corpse was younger, a hair past thirteen. Hollow brown eyes stared from a bruised and battered head. A bullet wound in the middle of the chest had brought quick and sudden death. But perhaps feeling cheated by their enemy's swift end, the killers had taken great delight in scalping and mutilating the young Indian.

Even though the body was blood-stained and slashed horribly, Carter had little trouble identifying Buffalo Hump. Not so long before, Carter had nursed the boy's battered feet.

"You must've been mighty afraid of this boy," Carter said, kneeling beside the limp figure. "Takes a special breed to carve a child up like this."

"He was a Comanche!" Farrell shouted. "You should've seen what they did to my brother Fitz!"

"And that justifies this butchery?" Carter asked. "Look at him, Farrell! He's hardly as tall as my second boy. He was mighty dangerous, all right."

"It comes of ridin' with bad company," Ben Copeland declared.

"Well, dying maybe does," Carter said as he got to his feet and glared at the riders. "But not this butchering. You call them savage! I wonder what you can call yourselves after what you've done this night."

Carter buried the older Indian across Ioni Creek. He and Brady took Buffalo Hump to the cliff and set him on a scaffold erected alongside his father.

"Nighthawk would be glad of the company," Walt Harper said, sadly staring off into the distance.

Carter walked to the edge of the cliff and began chanting the Comanche mourning song. Brady gripped his father's arm and shook as a haunting wind seemed to reach out and tear at their faces.

"Rest easy, old friends," Carter said finally. "Your pain is over."

Not so mine, Carter thought as he rode homeward with his son. I fear that it's only beginning.

CHAPTER 7

SPRING arrived in high fashion. The yellow seas of buffalo grass were overnight painted green and alive. Seas of wildflowers swept the hillsides. A chorus of songbirds greeted the morning sun, and the white oaks and willows put on their April finery.

There was no further news of Johnny nor the Comanches. The farms and ranches settled down to plant crops or round up cattle. Carter devoted himself to tending to the thousand-odd chores that came with the close of winter. Shingles wanted replacing, and shutters had to be opened. Chicken coops and hog pens would be patched. A count would be made of the cattle, and calves would be branded.

Carter took Brady and J. T. with him into the southern hills to hunt mustangs. In all, twenty wild horses were roped and driven to the work corral back on Ioni Creek. Two months' labor remained of gentling and breaking those ponies to saddle, but their arrival brought a needed distraction for the entire family.

As the weather grew warmer, the toil grew fierce. Working the cattle was a wearying, dusty task, and tending the horses wasn't much better. So toward the end of the day, Carter would drag Brady and J. T. up the creek to where a deep pool formed. They would shed their clothes and enjoy a brief swim and a bit of rare foolishness.

Sometimes J. T. would ride to the house and fetch Nathan and Richmond. Other times some boys from neighboring farms and ranches, or passengers from the stagecoach, would join in. The boys wrestled and splashed away their fatigue. Carter listened to the laughter and tried to forget his worries.

It wasn't easy. As he gazed at Brady's broadening shoulders, at the new confidence swelling the boy's chest, Carter realized how old fourteen could seem. He had been an orphan at fourteen. And though Brady had only had his birthday the week before, there was no disputing the fact that the boy seemed older.

Nate, too, had celebrated a birthday. The squirmy lump of mischief and blond hair was eight now, and when splashing through the shallows with Nate on his shoulders, Carter couldn't help recalling how he'd carried Johnny in a like manner not so very long ago.

Lord, keep him safe, Carter silently prayed again and again.

After swimming, the exhausted young cowboys would sprawl on the grassy hillside and listen to their father spin a tale of the old days. Hadley Copeland would listen uneasily to stories of hunting buffalo with Comanches, and some of the stagecoach passengers shrank in terror at the mere mention of Indians.

Hadley's younger brother Moss summed those yarns up best, perhaps.

"It's good to hear about how things used to be," the twelve-year-old told Carter. "Pa didn't come out here till things were pretty tame."

Tame? Carter wondered. The land seemed as rebellious as ever, and with Jasper Farrell riding the river every day, the return of violence seemed never more than a stone's throw away.

In town, folks continued to mutter accusations at the Ross family. Carter tried his best to ignore them, but he could read their effect in Hope's eyes, on the faces of the boys.

"What else can I do?" he asked as he worked the mustangs. "I am what I am. I can't hunt my own brother!"

He shook off the anger and buried himself in the work.

Horses still brought a fine price in Weatherford each spring, and the new crop of mustangs was most promising. Most rebelled a bit at first, then gradually accepted their fate. Only a spotted mare continued to buck Carter's efforts.

There's always one that resists, Carter told himself. Some respond to gentling, to a lick of salt and a pat on the flanks. Others need a firm hand, a bit more rope, a lash at times. In the end, though, all wear the saddle.

He couldn't help feelilng it was the very method Mackenzie had used on the Comanches. Coax 'em, make promises, give presents and provide rations. Then if they remain on the plains, fight 'em till they're dead or defeated.

Carter couldn't help admiring the defiant mare. Perhaps it reminded him of Johnny, of old Walt and himself. But in the end all of them would break—or die.

It wasn't a pleasant thought, and it brought a great frown to Carter's face. As he washed for supper, he imagined himself running wild and free like those mustangs, eluding each lasso, every trap, until finally a rawhide lariat choked the resistance from him, and he felt the sting of a whip and the fiery touch of a branding iron.

"Pa, you all right?" J. T. asked as Carter winced.

"Sure, son," Carter said, leading the youngster toward the kitchen.

But he remained silent throughout the meal, and afterward Hope asked him to help dry the dishes. That was normally Nathan's duty, and it was unlike her to release any of the children from a regular chore. Nate didn't object in the least, and Carter, reading an urgency in her eyes, readily agreed.

"You didn't invite me to dry china plates to improve my health," Carter said as he dried the plates and placed them on the appropriate shelf in Hope's walnut hutch.

"No," she confessed. "I had something else in mind."

"Such as?"

"How much longer will the count take?"

"We're through," Carter explained. "The tally sheets have to be added, but the counting's been done."

"And the repairs to the coop?"

"Another day or so.

"What about the horses?"

"Oh, they're a far cry from ready," Carter told her. "We have a while, though. I'm not worried."

"Could you finish without the boys?"

"Why?"

"I think they should start going into Palo Pinto for school."

"Oh, Hope," he grumbled, shaking his head. "We've talked of this before. They can learn here what they need to know. Brady's got twice the head for figures of any man in town, and he reads far better than that old hypocrite Hollings."

"Mrs. Hollings has a small library, Carter. There are books aplenty for Brady to read. It's not just for the books I want him to go, though. You've got a fine hand with livestock, Carter, and you weave magic with horses. Even so, we have a hard time making a go of things. How will this place ever support four grown boys with families?"

"I never figured it would."

"Nor I. One will stay here to take over the ranch. The rest will make their way in town or buy their own place."

"So it would seem likely."

"How will they survive if they don't learn how to deal with other people, Carter? They'll need the goodwill of their neighbors, a bank loan to help purchase land, schools to educate, and churches in which to worship. Who will they marry, one of our old sows? It's time they met other youngsters."

"I'm not so sure," Carter argued. "We're not like other people. I don't know that I feel right about sending the boys, especially Nate, into town to be preached at. Now they know who they are, and they're proud of it. I hate to see those other kids peel the hide off 'em, break their hearts with words and tales."

"They're strong enough."

"Are they? Know how many times I've seen you cry when you get back from town? You think I'm elsewhere, and I've never said anything, but it tears at me to see you so sad, Hope. I wouldn't wish that for the boys."

"Sooner or later they'll have to live with these people, Carter. We have to join the community. Otherwise our children will wind up as lost and alone as Johnny."

It was a sobering thought, but Carter would not allow the boys to start school.

"Try it a month," Hope urged. "A week even."

"No," Carter argued. "If I pulled 'em out then, it would seem like we were cowards. I never backed down from a tangle with anybody."

"I know," she said, resting her head on his shoulder. "I wish it were otherwise. You've done a lot of bleeding that might have been avoided."

Maybe so, Carter thought, but a man who never makes a stand has no roots. He just blows in the summer wind. That was not the legacy he wished for his sons.

And so the boys remained at the ranch. J. T. and Brady tended the cattle and occasionally helped with the mustangs. Nathan fed the hogs and chickens, and Richmond, fast approaching his fifth birthday now, helped his mother in the garden or looked after little Rachel when the girl would allow it.

More news came soon of new cavalry sweeps across the Llano. Stragglers were ridden down and rounded up. Others, starved or frozen during the ravages of winter, were found dead by freighters or stagecoaches crossing the plains. Except for the infrequent disappearance of a horse or cow upriver, no sign of Comanches could be found near Ross's Gap.

Then, on a storm-swept night the first week of April, wolves took to howling across the creek. The noise unnerved the whole family, and Carter set off to investigate. With a

Winchester in his hands he approached the creek cautiously. Clouds masked the moon, and the awful wailing was all the more eerie for lack of light.

Carter shuddered. Up ahead a shadow moved across the trail. Brady and J. T. kept a careful watch back at the house, but Carter couldn't rid himself of the notion that great peril awaited his family. He cocked the rifle and waited to fire. A twig snapped, and he tensed. Then an eerie pale horse trotted forward. Carter raised his rifle, then stepped aside to allow the riderless horse to pass.

"You by yourself?" a familiar voice asked from the darkness.

"Johnny?" Carter gasped.

"Are you alone, Cart?"

"Yes," Carter said, stepping out from the safety of an oak. "Come along, you fool. I could've shot you."

"I wouldn't find that too pleasant," Johnny said, slowly joining his brother. Even in the faint light Carter could tell his brother was soaked to the skin and worn to a frazzle. The two gripped each other, and Johnny collapsed. Carter helped him rise, and the brothers struggled along to the house.

"It's all right," Carter called when they reached the house. "It's Johnny."

J. T. and Brady rushed outside to help their uncle along, and Carter left the boys to bear Johnny to the door. Hope was already fetching linens. She retreated a step when the light met Johnny's hollow face, illuminating his sunken cheeks and frayed hair.

"I've been a long time riding," Johnny whispered. "A long time."

"And now you're home," Carter said, leading him along to the room Brady and J. T. shared.

"Home," Johnny mumbled as he fell face first into the bed. "Home. Ma, is that you?" He then gently called out a string of Comanche phrases as Carter struggled to peel the dingy deerskin rags from his brother's shivering body.

"J.T., his horse is out there somewhere," Carter said, gripping the boy's shoulders. "Get it unsaddled and rubbed down. Make sure it's in the barn, out of sight."

"Yes, sir," J. T. said, scrambling off to do just that.

"Brady?"

"Pa?" the older boy responded.

"Help your mother ready a bath. Then see about making yourself a bed, will you? You don't mind your uncle sharing your room, do you?"

"Not if we can get a story or two in the bargain," Brady said, grinning.

"Seems a fair price," Carter agreed, waving the boy along.

Soon a tub of water was made ready, and Carter carried Johnny along to the kitchen. Hope drew the children along to their beds while Carter washed away a month's grime from the weary, dark-haired young man whose thin frame and solemn gaze did indeed seem to be that of a ghost.

"You've had a hard time indeed," Carter commented as he cleansed a dozen wounds. "Are you home to stay?"

"No," Johnny mumbled. "There were too many soldiers on the Llano. They caught up with us. Many died. The rest scattered."

"Runs Long?" Carter asked. "Owl Eyes?"

"With Walt," Johnny explained. "The old man knows how to keep them in the shadows. They'll be safe."

"And the others?"

"Don't know, Carter. So many dead. Just boys, you know. Buffalo Hump was the first. So many."

"I know," Carter said, remembering the war, the charges across hillsides littered with dead—graycoats and bluecoats mixed like one of his mother's quilts. A sea of dead, he'd often called it, with blood enough to drown a nation.

"My horse?" Johnny babbled.

"Tended," Carter assured him. "Nothing will be left to chance. Don't worry. You're safe here."

"Safe?"

Carter read a great bitterness surging through his brother's chest. What nightmare had Johnny endured? It was impossible to know, and Carter would never ask. That much all warriors shared, no matter what their wars or when. Killing and dying were best left forgotten, even if that was seldom possible.

Once Johnny was bathed and his wounds were dressed, Carter produced a clean nightshirt. The bedraggled young man, the Gray Ghost who'd spread terror across the Texas frontier, took to bed and snored away.

"It's not safe, his staying," Hope warned as Carter sat beside her on the side of their bed. "He's in danger now, and so are we. There are far too many visitors through here these days."

"He has no other place to go," Carter said. "I won't send him away."

"He'll go on his own," she whispered. "He knows the soldiers or Jasper Farrell or someone else will come in time."

"So long as he grows strong, has time to recover, I really don't care."

"Carter?"

"Yes, dear."

"Have you ever considered the best way to save his life might be to turn him over to the soldiers at Ft. Griffin?"

"That might keep his hide from being filled with bullets, but it wouldn't mean he'd live, Hope. To cage a man like Johnny would be to cut out his heart. I've searched my mind for a way to help, but I've found none. All we can do, I suppose, is help ease the pain and then wait for him to ride off again."

She nodded sadly, and Carter put out the lamp. The night soon swallowed them—doubts, worries, and all.

CHAPTER 8

Carter hadn't slept soundly since riding off to war. Back then the snap of a twig meant anything from a Yank scout to a regimental attack. He'd been responsible for other lives, and his ears would respond to the slightest movement. Upon returning home he'd had Hope and the little ones to protect, to shield from prowling wolves, raiding Indians, and renegade whites. Strangely enough, while the other ranches and farms bounding the Brazos had most feared Comanche attack, Carter had understood the small bands of raiders angered at settlers carving up the buffalo valleys. Near-starved wolves and deserters of three armies—Yank, reb, and the new frontier cavalry—were too unpredictable. Often they would strike out in fury at simple folk for no good reason.

"World's gone crazy!" Walt Harper had growled when he and Carter had buried a pair of boys who'd left their parents at the way station long enough to swim away a sunny summer afternoon. Renagades had killed the pair for their clothes.

The world's gone crazy again, Carter often told himself. Maybe it's always been that way.

Such notions came and went between dreams of better days—and nightmares of worse. Through his mind rolled scenes of laughter, winter nights gathered around a twilight fire, Hope at his side, and the children huddled close. He heard J. T.'s soft voice amid the guitar's gentle melody.

Carter, in his dream, was leading Hope around the floor of the Cashwell's barn at an April dance when a loud cry shook him from his slumber. Instantly he was on his feet and rushing out of the room. A second cry drew him to the small room shared by Brady and J. T. On Brady's bed Johnny sat

74

up, shivering as he cried out a third time. He tore apart his nightshirt and clawed at his chest. J. T. and Brady stood in their bedclothes at the foot of the bed, their eyes full of terror. Carter passed them without speaking and gripped his brother by the shoulders.

"Johnny, it's all right," Carter said, calmly breaking the grip of the midnight terror even as he had in the weeks following their father's death. "Johnny?"

Johnny slowly ceased his shivering. His eyes opened wide, and a nervous grin replaced the terrified frown on his face.

"You're all right," Carter said, sitting beside his brother on the bed. "You're safe."

"I was . . . back on . . . the Llano," Johnny stammered more to the boys than to their father. "The soldiers . . . came . . . once more."

"They're not here now," Carter whispered.

"They will come again," Johnny said, staring at the long red tears in his chest. "I must go."

"You're going nowhere," Carter objected. "No one will bother you here."

Johnny shook his head and rolled off the edge of the bed. He stood tall and straight, the shreds of his shirt dangling below his knees. Even now the ghosts of the nightmare haunted him. Then, as Brady lit a lamp, the shadows of the dream departed.

"The soldiers chase me even in my dreams," Johnny said, drawing the boys close. "I've fought them long and hard. Always I escape, and always they return."

"Pa's right," J. T. said, glancing over at Carter. "They can't hurt you here. We won't let 'em."

Johnny stroked the younger boy's cheek and shuddered. Gradually the fear left, and all three brightened. Carter thought to leave them, but when he stepped toward the door, Brady's eyes drew him back.

"Tell us about it, Uncle Johnny," J. T. pleaded. "Tell us about the soldiers."

"It's not a tale for boys," Carter said, reading Johnny's reluctance.

"I'm fourteen," Brady objected. "How old was Buffalo Hump?"

"They know?" Johnny asked.

"Farrell brought the boy here," Carter explained. "We set him on a scaffold beside his father."

"Thank you," Johnny said, gripping Carter's wrists. "It's weighed upon my heart that we left him behind."

Johnny then took a deep breath and described the terrible ordeal of the Llano, of camps torn apart by hard-riding squads of bluecoat cavalry. He spoke of boys and girls torn from their mothers' arms, of warriors standing defiantly with only their bare arms for weapons. The scene was truly terrifying, and the boys' eyes turned dark and anxious.

When Johnny finished, silence draped the room. In the shadows cast on the walls by heads and elbows, Carter saw dancing ponies and flashing lances. Brady leaned against his father's side, and Carter noted the boy's trembling arms.

"There aren't any soldiers here," Carter finally said. "It's time we all took to our beds. Morning will come early."

Brady slowly crawled over to where his mattress lay beside the window. J. T. slid over and touched Carter lightly on the arm before moving along to the far bed. Johnny stared out the window at the distant stars, and Carter sighed. Only time and peace would keep the ghosts at bay.

For a time it seemed that peace would come. Johnny devoted his days to building a second corral and working the mustangs. Brady and J. T. felled live oaks and junipers, then trimmed oak bark and split the bare logs into rails. It was tiring work, but it drew the boys and their dark-skinned uncle close.

"Just like old times," Johnny told Carter as they constructed the corral. "We sweated away many a spring."

"Yes," Carter agreed. "It's the way spring should be passed, with good work and family."

Johnny cracked a smile, and for a while those earlier months of terror and blood faded into memory. Days came and went, and the brothers devoted their afternoons to frolicking with the boys down at the creek, to wrestling and racing ponies and remembering.

Lurking in the shadows was the unspoken truth of Johnny's recent activities. And when the Copeland boys or the crew from the way station appeared at the creek, Johnny would slip into the trees and vanish.

Far worse were the occasional visits of Jasper Farrell. Farrell often brought news of the cavalry's campaign out on the Llano, and he especially delighted in tormenting Carter Ross with tales of small bands ridden into the dust.

Farrell's visits unnerved Hope.

"I wish that awful man would leave us be," she told Carter. "Why does he torment us?"

"Some men let the hate inside eat them up," Carter replied. "That's how it is for Farrell. He and his brother used to have a fine herd of longhorns and a fair string of cow ponies. The stock's wandered off over the years, and now there's little to show for a lifetime of labor."

"I can't escape the feeling that he knows Johnny's here."

"No, we're quite careful around strangers."

"Are you? The way you two scream and shout when you race those mustangs through the creek would draw anybody's attention. Even with his hair clipped short and dressed in your clothes, neighbors know who he is. It's not safe, Carter, not for him or for us."

"He's my brother," Carter argued. "He has a right to be here. What's more, he's been a big help with the horses."

"And with the boys," she said, smiling. "That changes nothing, though. Have you considered what will happen if Jasper Farrell arrives some day when Johnny's out in the open? Farrell won't bother saying hello before shooting. Can you live with that? Can the boys? And how will our neighbors respond?"

The questions left Carter cold and hollow. He didn't want to consider such an event. And when May arrived, he readied ten ponies for the market at Weatherford. The journey to market and the sale would take half a week. Brady would come along to help with the stock. J. T. reluctantly agreed to stay and help Johnny finish the corral.

The trip to market proved a success. A buyer from Ft. Worth bought all ten horses and promised an equal price for five more come summer. Some of the cash was swapped for needed supplies, including a bolt of new fabric for Hope and some stick candy for the children. A pair of boots, promised Nathan for his birthday, was added.

When they passed through Palo Pinto, Carter felt suspicious eyes watching them pass. Two town boys waved cheerfully at Brady, only to be drawn aside by stone-faced mothers. Brady's smile fell, and a sour taste filled Carter's mouth. Hope, as always, was right about the neighbors. But Carter wasn't convinced Johnny's departure would change anything.

In the weeks that followed, Carter never felt quite the same warmth as back in April. The boys noticed the change, too. They steered visitors clear of the house, and often warned of approaching riders. With school out for the hot summer months, the river and creeks abounded with youngsters, and Johnny kept closer to home or joined old Walt, Runs Long, and Owl Eyes atop Antelope Mountain. Brady and J. T. rode the distant hills with the Copeland boys when not supplying fresh vegetables to the way station.

One afternoon as the boys dipped lines into Ioni Creek, Carter joined them in the shade of a tall white oak.

"Heard the news?" an eager Hadley Copeland asked.

J. T.'s scowl hinted the news would not be welcome, but Hadley couldn't be restrained.

"Quannah Parker's given up!" Hadley exclaimed. "Pa says that'll be the end of the raids. There's a Comanche or two still loose, but the cavalry rounds a few more up each week, and the rest'll give up or else wander across the wrong farm.

I heard some of those old buff hunters've posted a bounty of ten dollars a head on the ones that're left. A few days back a pair of Comanches got shot up on the Clear Fork."

"Oh?" Carter asked nervously.

"Just young ones. Pa says they were likely with the bunch that hit our place back in the winter."

A chill crept through Carter's chest. He imagined the youthful faces of Runs Long and Owl Eyes.

"Oh, I'm sorry, Mr. Ross," Hadley suddenly said, backing away. "You know some of those Comanches, don't you?"

Carter searched the fifteen-year-old's eyes for traces of sincerity. Jasper Farrell would have made such a comment and grinned sourly. Hadley Copeland seemed a little shaken, and Carter trusted the boy's words as genuine.

"I can't find much pleasure in anybody's dying nowadays," Carter finally replied. "I saw too many in the war, I guess."

"Sure," Hadley responded with downcast eyes. "I never thought about . . . well . . . I guess I have a mouth runs a bit too long sometimes. Ma says as much."

Carter managed a grin, then set off for the house. He met his brother behind the barn and shared the news. Johnny responded by walking off into the trees and staring sadly toward the north. Carter followed and joined Johnny atop a large boulder.

"Have you seen Runs Long and Owl Eyes?" Carter asked. "The dead ones on the Clear Fork were young."

"They are well," Johnny assured his brother. "As well as a Kwahadi can be in this hour of death."

"If Quannah has gone in," Carter whispered, "it's all over."

"Yes," Johnny muttered. "All but the dying."

Johnny then chanted somberly, and Carter knew the world was again turning. Soon events would sweep through the hills and tear them apart.

The hunt was Hope's idea.

"I've never seen so many downcast faces," she declared.

"And I'm tired of frying bacon and stewing beef. Why don't you see if you can scare up a deer?"

Carter met the notion with no enthusiasm, but J. T. jumped to his feet and howled. Little Nate pleaded to go along, and even Brady seemed eager to escape the confinement of the house amid a fierce spell of June heat.

"There is good country for deer along the river," Johnny said, grinning at Carter. He nodded, and it was settled. They spent a day cleaning rifles and readying supplies, then set off toward the river.

Carter had hunted there the first time as a boy little older than Nathan. At eight he had had to rest his rifle on a rock to steady the shot. Later he'd brought Johnny there. It was a well-remembered spot, and Carter was happy to share the stories of earlier hunts with the boys around an evening campfire.

The next morning Johnny spotted deer tracks down at the river. After making a brief prayer to the spirit of the deer, he led the way through tangled brush that tore at arms and knees, across sharp rocks, and past the wicked thorny limbs of mesquite trees. Finally they located a small doe in a nest of briars. Johnny nodded for Brady to take the shot, but Brady stepped aside so J. T. could fire instead. The twelve-year-old steadied his rifle, cocked the hammer, and fired.

The shot resounded through the hollow and sent two other deer flying to cover. J. T. had sharp eyes and true aim, and the bullet found its mark. The doe fell to one shoulder, then collapsed.

"Fine shot, son," Carter said, patting J. T. on his back. "Let's get her dressed and to your ma. She'll bake us some cornbread to go with venison steaks, I'll bet."

J. T. glowed, and Brady grinned broadly. Nate, happy to be a part of the hunt, outraced them both to the fallen deer. It was Johnny who made the throat cut and began skinning the animal, though.

As they dressed the kill, Johnny spun tales of other hunts,

of setting after the buffalo with Nighthawk in better days. The boys responded with stories of their own. Brady spoke of bagging quail, and J. T. recounted shooting a pair of plump rabbits back in early autumn. Then a rifle shot from down the river hushed them.

"Pa?" Brady cried in alarm as other shots followed. A volley answered, and for a brief few moments Carter drew his sons to cover and shuddered as visions of Tennessee battlefields rushed through his head. The firing soon died, though, and silence reigned again over the river bottom.

"The Copeland place is down that way," J. T. pointed out. "Moss said they've lately had trouble with rustlers."

"Pa, Jasper Farrell was camped down by the river a mile from Hadley's house," Brady added. "Don't you think we ought to have a look?"

Nate cowered behind a boulder, and J. T. clung to his uncle.

"I think I'd better have a look," Carter told them.

"I'll come, too," Johnny declared.

"You'll stay here out of sight," Carter instructed. "Someone's got to look after the boys."

Brady thought to object, then stopped. Maybe the boy could read Carter's thoughts. It was Johnny faced the greatest danger. The youngsters would keep *him* safe.

Carter mounted his horse and rode a mile and a half down the Brazos before encountering Jasper Farrell and the Copelands. Hadley and Moss stood pale-faced and frozen beside a pair of deerskin-clad corpses. Their dark, braided hair and manner of dress told Carter instantly they were Comanche.

Farrell gabbed away, poking the bodies with the toe of his boot and laughing loudly as he removed a necklace of eagle claws from the nearest one. Copeland didn't appear to share either the amusement or the inclination to strip the bodies.

"It's all over," Hadley called as Carter arrived. "Shoot, they didn't even have any bullets for their rifles."

"We didn't know that," Moss cried, shuddering as Farrell peeled a shirt from the first body.

"Do you have to do that?" Copeland complained as Farrell continued removing clothing.

"Listen, friend, nobody down here's payin' me any bounty, you know," the former scout explained. "These things bring a fair price from travelers. Sort of a curiosity nowadays."

"Bloodstained?" Moss asked, shielding his eyes.

"Oh, that's the best kind," Farrell told the boys. "Friend of mine up near Ft. Griffin sells the ears, too. Why I've known toes and fingers to fetch a price. These ones are too young, of course."

Hadley raced off into the trees and became sick. Moss dropped to his knees and covered his eyes.

Carter stared grimly at the corpses. Lying still, their sides and chests torn apart by rifle blasts, the dead Comanches appeared all too harmless. Neither could have been much older than young Moss. That knowledge weighed heavily on the boys. It might not have been so bad had not Farrell stripped the bodies. Naked, their skin stretched tautly over bones, the two half-starved young bodies told a story of desperate flight and great hardship.

"We tracked 'em here," Copeland said, turning to Carter. "I had a steer stolen. We only saw their backs and the steer there, slaughtered and cut ûp for supper. If I'd known they were so young . . ."

"Don't let it worry you," Carter said, kneeling beside the young faces and gently closing their eyes. "You put an end to their hunger. I don't think they'd find you at fault."

"Fault?" Farrell objected. "Why, they're Comanche, aren't they?"

"Not anymore," Carter said sadly.

Farrell drew out a knife and turned it toward the closest one, but Copeland and his boys had seen enough. Moss screamed, and Copeland kicked the knife aside.

"This is my land, Farrell, and I won't have anyone scalped here!" Copeland barked.

"You don't understand their ways!" Farrell complained. "You got to mark the dead some, elsewise they . . ."

"It's you doesn't understand!" Hadley interrupted, raising his rifle. "You do any cutting, I'll shoot you right in the face." Farrell dropped his jaw and gazed anxiously at the young rifleman. Haldey was deadly serious. Farrell gathered up the necklace and the scraps of deerskin, then made his way to where his horse was tethered to a small pine.

"I'll send someone out to bury 'em," Copeland promised as he waved his sons toward him.

"Leave that to me," Carter said. "They won't need much of a hole."

"No," Copeland agreed. "Ever see 'em before?"

"I haven't traveled with Indians since before the war," Carter said, staring hard at his neighbor. "You shouldn't believe everything Farrell says. He has a powerful hate, and it sours him toward life."

"I told you he wasn't Indian, Pa," Hadley said.

"You never ride with us," Copeland said bitterly. "What's a man to think?"

"Maybe that some haven't got the heart for killing children," Carter replied. "Or for traveling in the company of Jasper Farrell."

"You know that's not why we set out."

"Maybe not," Carter grumbled. "But whatever the reason, it brought you here."

The Copelands turned, mounted their horses, and returned home. Carter began scratching out a shallow grave in the hard ground above the river. He'd barely begun when Johnny and the boys arrived.

"It's best you boys stay where you are," Carter warned.

Johnny understood immediately and drew Nate aside. Brady and J. T. continued on. They stared at the young corpses, then quickly dashed off to Nate's side.

"Take the meat to your mother," Johnny suggested. "We'll be along."

Carter nodded, and the youngsters headed south.

"I know this one," Johnny said, touching the cold, lifeless chin of the younger Comanche. "Once he and his brother rode with Nighthawk. He was called Winter Rabbit."

"They were nearly starved," Carter mumbled. "The world has grown dark indeed."

"Carter, I must stay no longer," Johnny said, drawing out a knife and joining in the digging.

"Johnny, there's no place for you out there. The Kiowas are finished. Quannah's given up. All that's left are confused boys and old people who haven't the strength to reach the reservation. You're my brother. You know horses. Stay with me and Hope, share our future."

"You forget Owl Eyes and Runs Long."

"They're young. They can learn new ways."

"I'm not. You say we're brothers, Carter. We are, but we're different. Look at me. I'm not white! Even if my skin was fair as yours is, I could never live in a house, cut my hair, and wear clothes all summer. I'll never be a white man."

"I don't make a very good one myself most of the time," Carter confessed.

They finished digging in silence. After laying the dead in a shallow trench, they covered the place with stones and walked to the river.

"My heart is heavy," Johnny admitted.

"Mine, too," Carter said, grasping his younger brother's hand.

"I know. It will be a cold summer."

Carter gazed skyward. The sun beat down mercilessly. Inside, though, a chill as fierce as any January blizzard gripped his heart. Yes, it would be a cold summer. And a long one.

CHAPTER 9

JOHNNY vanished like a wisp of smoke. With him went three horses—two pintos and a gray gelding.

"It's best you report 'em stolen," Walt said. "Was Johnny's idea. Make it easier with other folk in case somebody reads the brands sometime."

"So now I'm to lie?" Carter asked.

"They were taken," old Walt pointed out. "It's a truth, isn't it?"

"No, Walt. Johnny knows anything I've ever owned is his for the asking."

"Then accept his gift, Cart. He knows as long as he stayed, you could never tear down that fence across the gap and be like other folks."

"He told you that?"

"It's true, isn't it? Now he's gone to find his fate, and it's time you started accepting yours."

Carter turned and stared sadly toward the west. And in his heart he spoke to the vanished brother and again prayed he would remain safe.

The first week in July a telegraph arrived in Palo Pinto from the Ft. Worth mustang buyer. In another week a broker in Weatherford would accept delivery of the five contracted horses. Carter turned his full attention to readying the animals, and in celebration of the sale, he loaded the whole family in a wagon and took them along to Weatherford.

The five ponies trailed along behind, watched by Brady and J. T. John Tyler Ross would turn thirteen on the home-ward leg of the trip, and the skinny, flaxen-haired boy jabbered endlessly about having a rifle of his own, a new felt hat, a full-sized saddle, and even a razor.

"That's pure foolishness," Brady remarked. "You've not got so much as a hair on your chin yet, little brother. Waste of good cash, that'd be."

"And what would you know about my chin, Brady?" J. T. asked. "I don't recall your asking me for a good-night kiss!"

"Who would?" Brady asked, laughing.

"So happens Kate Reed did just last week. She says pretty soon I'll be shaving."

"Must be blind, that girl, to take after a beanpole like you."

The boys went on bickering most of the journey. Carter and Hope exchanged smiles, and Nate entertained Rich and Rachel with a fine imitation of the older boys. Once they were in Weatherford, the horses were delivered, and Hope headed for the large mercantile.

She had filled three boxes with supplies when Carter joined her. Brady and J. T. scurried about in search of something to buy. Carter had rewarded each of them with a shiny silver dollar for their diligent labors. Rachel cradled a rag doll and followed her mother from shelf to shelf. Nate and Rich huddled beside the candy jar.

"I know you?" the clerk asked when Carter piled the needed items on the front counter.

"Don't think so," Carter answered. "We're from west of here."

"Palo Pinto County," the clerk said, grinning. "I never forget a face. You'd be the Kincaids."

"No," Carter said, shaking his head. "Carter Ross."

"Oh, yes," the clerk muttered as he tallied the bill. "I remember. You're a halfbreed as I recall."

"I look it?" Carter asked, removing his hat so that his light hair fell across his forehead.

"I remember now," the clerk said, rubbing his chin. "Your pa took a Comanche squaw to his cabin. That's how I recollect it. You rode with those Indians, raided farms and such."

The others in the store gazed warily at Carter. Some backed out the door. One woman cursed at little Nate.

"Butchers," another added.

"Tally the bill," Carter said angrily. "We'll be on our way."

"Not far enough for our taste," a tall, thin-faced man declared.

"Quick!" Carter growled as the others collected in an angry cluster.

"Don't you take that manner with me," the clerk complained. "It's none too healthy in this town for a Comanche breed. I wouldn't act so uppity if I was you."

"You want my business or not?" Carter asked. "There are other folks run mercantiles."

The store's owner stepped out from his office and frowned.

"Got some kind of trouble here, Jeff?" the owner called.

"Just these breeds makin' trouble," the clerk answered.

"Jeff, you go walk down to the stable and back, think over whether you need this job or not," the owner replied angrily. "Now, sir, I'd ask you to excuse my clerk here. He's young and hasn't been with us long. Elsewise he'd know better than to deal out names like bad aces in a card game."

"He's ridden with Comanches, Mr. Shelton," one of the women remarked.

"Jeff tell you that?" Shelton said, laughing. "He'd not know a Comanche from a bedbug. As for this gentleman, I sent my nephew off to ride with him to Tennessee. This man wore the gray four years, friends, and he need never explain himself to anyone in my place of business."

The others were taken a bit by surprise and withdrew in embarrassment.

"You buried my sister's boy at Selma," Shelton explained. "Bob McLemore."

"A fine boy," Carter said, recalling the young cavalryman.

"I know of your father, too," Shelton whispered. "Most folks here now don't recall the Second Cavalry. These newcomers and their high-handed ways gall me. But they're the future. I'd keep my eyes on the road going home. Jeff's got a big mouth and a sharp temper. I'm sorry you came across him in my store."

Carter nodded, then paid for the goods. He and the boys then loaded up the wagon and headed west.

"I thought we were going to visit the saddle shop," J. T. objected. "I got my birthday tomorrow, remember?"

"I remember," Carter said, urging the boy along. "I'd feel better making evening camp a little farther from town's all."

J. T. read his father's worried eyes and swallowed any complaints.

That night Carter made camp halfway to Palo Pinto near a small spring. He kept a fire burning all night in spite of the sweltering July weather.

"Just once I wish we could be like other folks," Hope complained when Carter rested his rifle beside his blankets.

"We're not."

"We could be," she said. "Johnny's gone. He knows he's out of place here. He can't find a way to bridge the gap, but we have to. For them," she added, pointing to the sleeping children.

The words echoed through Carter's head for an hour. He stared up at the stars overhead and wondered how it would ever be possible. He didn't want to be like Jasper Farrell or Ben Copeland. As for the children, they were ever so much finer than the brash young fools in Palo Pinto.

Like others? Carter asked himself. We're better. Even so, he worried about the future . . . and the present. Only the past tended itself.

CHAPTER 10

THAT next morning, Carter had the boys up early, gathering firewood to place on the dim embers of the campfire. He sent Brady down the road to buy eggs and a slab of bacon off a farmer, then prepared to tend to the cooking chores himself. J. T. gazed in expectation each time his name was called, but Carter withheld his birthday greetings. J. T. grew increasingly anxious, and the other boys grinned with pleasure whenever he stomped around the fire.

"Know what day it is?" he finally asked Carter.

"Tuesday, I believe," Carter answered. "Might be Wednesday. You know I can't keep track when I'm on the road. Ask your ma when she wakes. She keeps account so she has you youngsters in church come Sunday."

Hope slept peacefully through sunrise, though, and J. T. fumed.

"It's nigh impossible for anybody to get some attention in this family," Carter overhead the boy mumble to the horses. "I'd be better off out on the Llano with Uncle Johnny."

Finally Carter could stand it no longer. He grabbed J. T., slung him over one shoulder, and carried him along to the fire. There he administered the traditional pounding and welcomed John Tyler Ross to his fourteenth year.

J. T.'s bottom might have stung a bit, but he never betrayed a hint of discomfort. His mother was awakened by the disturbance, and she started off the celebration by presenting him with a new cotton shirt and leather vest.

By the time Brady returned with the makings for breakfast, other presents had been presented, including a deer rifle carefully concealed in the bed of the wagon.

"I thought you'd best have that little pinto pony we kept back at the corral as well," Carter told the boy. "Walt's made you a saddle. As for the boots, I fear you'll have to wait for Christmas."

"If your foot grows as big as your mouth, I've got an old pair in the tack room," Brady added.

"And the razor?" J. T. asked.

"That'll wait a couple of Christmases," Nate said, laughing.

Carter then busied himself frying bacon and eggs while the boys saddled horses and hitched the team to the wagon. Once the last of the food was devoured and the plates were scrubbed clean, Carter waved Nate, Rich, and little Rachel aboard the wagon. He helped Hope up onto the seat and took the reins. Moments later he had the wagon rolling up the road toward Palo Pinto. Brady and J. T. followed along behind.

A little after noon they passed through town. Few of the townfolk bothered to wave or even nod a head. When Carter stopped to give the horses a drink at the watering trough outside the livery, rotund Frank Walters frowned and waved them along.

"I know we're far from fast friends, Walters," Carter said with a scowl, "but you surely wouldn't begrudge my horses a drink in the middle of July. Lords knows I've brought back a horse or two that's thrown its rider over the years, and I don't recall ever asking so much as two bits for my effort."

"Water your animals and be gone with you," the liveryman grumbled. "I won't have my reputation spoiled by trading with you Rosses."

Others were equally unpleasant. Hope was stunned. Finally she ordered Carter to halt the wagon. She trotted over to the church and returned with Reverend Hollings and his wife.

"The Comanches have returned," she explained. "They burned the Rileys' barn and made off with a dozen horses."

"Others have had like trouble," the preacher explained.

"Jonathan Riley took an arrow through his leg. Boy's not yet eight years old. It's unclear whether the leg can be saved."

"It's well known where your sympathies lie, Mr. Ross," Mrs. Hollings added. "Ed Riley says the raiders headed straight up Ioni Creek toward your place with the stolen stock."

"Ioni Creek leads to lots of places," Carter grumbled. "We've been in Weatherford the whole time. I'm grieved to hear of the Riley lad, but it's not in my power to heal the sick or change what's done."

"No, that's in other hands," Reverend Hollings declared. "Hope, I'm certain the Rileys would appreciate any help you might provide. They're nearer to you than town, and Ruth will have her hands full with a lame boy and three other youngsters."

"I'll cook up a ham," Hope promised. "I'm certain the boys can give Ed a hand with his chores if it's needed."

"Bless you," Mrs. Hollings said, managing a smile. "Perhaps after all we've misjudged you."

Carter nodded, more out of gratitude for Hope's restored smile than for any praise directed his way. He never failed to help a neighbor when asked, but in truth, he preferred to tend his own business.

They continued along out of town then, swinging west toward the opening in the Palo Pinto Mountains named for Carter's father. The sight of Antelope Mountain, of the familiar creeks and ravines leading to Ross's Gap, brought a warmth to Carter. It was always good to turn homeward.

In the middle of the afternoon the wagon finally lumbered through the narrow pass and approached the rail fence across the gap. To Carter's surprise, a hole twenty feet wide had been torn from the fence. The smoking ashes of the missing rails were stacked in a bonfire a hundred yards away.

"What's happened here, Carter?" Hope asked in alarm.

"Something's been burned," he explained. "I can't tell what it could have been. There are tracks heading northwest, toward the Copeland place."

"Two sets," Brady said, pointing them out. The first trail was carved in the dry sandy soil by shod horses. The second was a mixture of unshod ponies and animals wearing shoes.

"Comanches," J. T. whispered with wide eyes. "Pa?"

Carter read the boy's thoughts. Johnny was likely with them. What's more, the Indian trail had come from the west, up Ioni Creek, then doubled back northwest.

"Pa, I don't understand," Brady said. "Why would they turn back on their tracks? It doesn't look like they were chased by the others."

No, Carter thought. More likely it was the other way around. As he poked among the smouldering embers, a small unburned deerskin pouch was uncovered. Carter stirred the ashes. He soon uncovered a fragment of shattered bone.

"What is it, Pa?" J. T. asked.

"Son, you take your ma and the little ones back home," Carter said, marching toward the sleek bay stallion J. T. was riding. "Brady, I want you to ride up and look in on Walt. Make sure he's well."

"Yes, sir," Brady answered, nudging his horse toward Antelope Mountain.

"Carter, you're not going out there alone, are you?" Hope asked.

"I thought you were the one always after me to join in things," he told her. Smiling as he exchanged places with J. T., Carter then urged the bay into a gallop and rode northwestward. It wasn't long before he detected a single pillar of smoke rising skyward from the Copeland ranch.

"Come on, boy," Carter said as he encouraged further effort from the horse. "Get me there before it's too late."

The animal seemed to sense the urgency and raced along the time-worn path. Soon they splashed through Ioni Creek and turned toward the Brazos—toward the Copeland place and ultimately to conflict.

As Carter rode, his ears detected the sounds of gunfire.

Up ahead the Copelands were likely firing at Kwahadi raid-ers. Johnny was likely there, too. Loud cries split the after-noon. Carter tried to determine what he would do when he arrived at the ranch. In his rush to get mounted, he had neglected to grab his rifle from the wagon. He wore a pistol on his hip, but he'd never been too good with a handgun, and he hadn't fought in close quarters since returning from the war.

And anyway, who could I fight? he asked himself. Not Johnny. For all the words that had passed between himself and the Copelands, Carter had no real hatred for them, and Hadley was as close to a friend as Brady ever had.

Carter drew in his reins and started to turn homeward. Something bade him to continue, though, and he nudged the horse into motion again.

The Copeland barn was nearly consumed by flames when Carter approached. Several rifles barked from the outbuild-ings, and three or four others fired from the windows of the house. The Comanches were busy rounding up horses from a corral and snatching chickens from two coops back of the kitchen. Carter searched for his brother. Johnny wasn't in sight. In truth, only a few Indians appeared at all, and they were very young. No one seemed to be firing at the house.

Carter, more confused than ever, searched the ground ahead. He saw no one, so he turned his horse toward the boys at the corral and charged them. Howling and firing his pistol, he sent the young Kwahadis scattering for cover. They managed to chase half the horses along as well. Carter didn't bother to stop them. Instead he rode back toward the house. The firing gradually died away, and Ben Copeland emerged from the door, clearly shaken by the unexpected raid on his ranch.

"They're gone," Carter announced, pointing toward the river. "I'm afraid they took some of your horses with 'em."

"We'll get 'em back," Copeland declared. "I never saw anything to top this, Ross. We just finished ridin' out with

Jasper Farrell. No sooner did we get back than those Indians are on us."

"It's Farrell's fault," Hadley said, appearing beside his father. "Was the burning."

"What burning?" Carter asked. "You mean my fence?"

"Some Comanches raided the Riley farm," Copeland explained. "Their boy Jonathan took an arrow in his leg. Most folks were pretty stirred up. We picked up a trail that took us across your place. There was a Comanche camped up in the hills. Had a bullet in his leg, and his horse wandered off. Farrell figured he knew where the rest were, so we took him along, built up a fire, and then . . ."

"You burned him," Carter said, trembling at the thought. "He didn't tell you anything, though."

"I don't think he even spoke English," Hadley said soberly. "It was awful. He screamed and hollered. Farrell only laughed."

"What will they do next?" Copeland asked. "You know 'em. You've lived with 'em. I need to know."

"I don't know what to tell you," Carter said, sighing.

"Sure, you do," Copeland objected. "You're bound to have a notion. Walt told us how you lost three horses yourself last week. And today you rode in and chased those Indians off. Tell us where to look. We'll go catch the snakes."

"It's not nearly so simple," Carter told them. "They could be anywhere from here to Mexico for all I know."

"Brady's always talking about how you could track a horned toad up a cliff," Hadley declared. "They were in too much of a hurry to hide the trail."

"I can't," Carter said. "I've got no heart for it. Besides, I have my own family to look after."

"You don't mean to leave?" Copeland asked in surprise. "We need your help!"

"Please, Mr. Ross," Hadley added.

"Have you so quickly forgotten those dead boys down at the river?" Carter asked the boy. "Leave it be."

"I can't," Hadley explained. "They burned my barn, shot at my ma, my brothers."

Carter nodded sadly. Wasn't it always to protect or avenge that a man rode out to deal death? Carter would have none of it. He turned his horse homeward and left the Copelands to their revenge. Smoke continued to rise from the burning timbers of the barn. Carter saw it even when he crossed the creek and rode to his house. It would soon fade, but the fighting would last.

When he reached the corral, J. T. eagerly took the horse.

"You figure I can run the pinto some?" the boy asked, pointing to the pony prancing spryly around the corral.

"Not today, son," Carter replied. "Another time."

J. T. glanced back at the smoke and nodded. Carter then continued on to the house. Hope was waiting for him, and they embraced.

"Is Brady back yet?" he asked.

"Yes," she told him. "Old Walt's fine, but he's worried. Jasper Farrell burned a Comanche on those rails."

"Yes, I know," Carter whispered. He then told her the rest.

A strange sense of foreboding gripped Carter that evening as he sat beside Hope at the supper table. The children took note of it. Their foreheads bore wrinkles, and the jesting and laughter that normally swept the evening table were absent. Outside brilliant streaks of orange and red illuminated the West Texas sky. And as the sun died in the distant hills, rifle shots echoed from the high cliffs overlooking the churning waters of the Brazos.

"Pa?" Brady asked.

"I know," Carter said, frowning. "Now let's finish our dinner."

"It's not the Copelands' again, is it?" J. T. asked.

"Well upriver," Carter judged. "Not our worry."

It was a lie, of course. Carter knew trouble had a way of spreading like a fever. Already it threatened to engulf them.

The future was always uncertain, but just now it seemed more terrifying than ever.

Carter passed a sleepless night. A dozen times he rose from his bed and drifted through the house. He touched the delicate hairs on little Rachel's head, and he replaced Richmond's stray hand beneath a sheet.

Brady and J. T. tossed and turned. Maybe Johnny had left some of his restlessness in the little room they had shared. More likely they worried, like their father, that the morrow would bring ill tidings. J. T. especially weighed on Carter's soul. The boy should have been racing his new pony, crying out to all the world the wonderful joy of being thirteen. Somehow that joy had been smothered by dark events, and Carter bore those events a heavy grudge.

Daybreak brought no relief. Jasper Farrell appeared before breakfast. Hadley Copeland and others escorted a Diamond C wagon toward town. A cowboy led two riderless horses along—a gray gelding and a smaller pinto pony.

"These the ones you had stolen?" Farrell asked.

"Two of 'em," Carter said, motioning for Brady to take the animals to the corral.

"We lost the other," Farrell explained. "Shootin' was heavy, and I fear we put too many holes in the stock. 'Course we shot a few Comanches, too."

The others laughed nervously.

"Pa, there's blood on the saddle," Brady called out as he led the horses off.

"Yeah, we got that ghost himself," Farrell boasted. "Always did think you put a good hand to your horses, Ross. That ghost must've appreciated your talents. He rode the gray himself. I never saw a man ride like that one. But we shot him just the same."

"Killed him?" J. T. asked.

"Not so lucky as that," Hadley said. "He isn't one of 'em we found this morning. The others are in the wagon."

"Have a look," Farrell suggested. "You might recognize one or two."

Carter thought to respond with anger, but he recalled the solemn faces of Owl Eyes and Runs Long. It was better to know if they might be among the fallen. Carter trotted to the wagon and gazed at the five figures laid elbow to elbow in the wagon. All were shot and scalped. The oldest was badly cut up. He might have been fourteen.

"Don't you ever catch any grown men?" Carter cried. "Look at 'em! There's a boy in there couldn't be more than ten!"

"He helped burn our barn," Ben Copeland said, riding in to join the others. "There was a boy younger than your eldest riding that pinto of yours. A man old enough to steal a horse is old enough to get himself shot."

"And butchered," Carter added. "I thought you didn't hold with such."

"Farrell says these Comanches believe they face eternity the way they die," Copeland said angrily. "I figure this'll put the fear in those that're left. A man with no hands can't shoot anybody else."

"How many of those boys carried rifles?" Carter asked. "I'd bet hardly a one of 'em. They look near starved. They were most likely after your chickens as much as your horses."

"If you'd ridden along, you might have talked 'em into giving up," Copeland suggested. "I don't speak their words. None of us do. There was little left but to shoot."

Carter shook his head and returned to the porch. Farrell waved the wagon along, then gleefully narrated the tale of a well-laid ambush. The Comanches had been trapped in a rocky stretch along the river and shot to pieces.

"There are others still down there, crawlin' around in the rocks," Farrell explained. "Some'll likely crawl to the top of the cliffs and die. A few'll hide out for a time, then creep in and steal a horse. I'll bet the ghost is still out there."

"He's got to be dead," Copeland argued. "I hit him twice myself. You saw the blood on that saddle. He's finished."

"He didn't appear an easy man to kill," Farrell declared. "I wouldn't expect him to die to suit you, Copeland. It's best we hound those that're left, flush 'em out, and end this business. You're a man to spot Comanche sign, Ross. Maybe you should have a look."

"You wouldn't want me along," Carter told them. "I never take knives to boys whose biggest crime is stealing a chicken or being born with red skin."

"You might ought to concern yourself with what folks're sayin'," Copeland advised. "You got a halfbreed brother, as I recall. Stayed around this place with your wife and boys when the war called you away. Back in '64 when Comanches burned farms and shot kids full of arrows, your place wasn't much troubled."

"I wouldn't know," Carter said, glaring at Copeland. "I was under arms at the time, off in Tennessee fighting for my flag. Not everybody stayed home."

Copeland's face flashed red, and for a moment Carter thought they might come to blows. Copeland seemed ready to dismount, but Carter Ross's cold gaze sent the tall rancher riding on.

"We'll be watchin' this place!" Farrell warned.

"I'd appreciate that," Carter replied. "Never objected when my neighbors took an interest in my welfare."

Farrell unleashed a string of curses, but Carter only laughed in reply.

"Watch yourself, Farrell!" Carter shouted. "You might come across a full-grown Indian one of these days. Your hair'd look awful pretty on a scalp pole."

Farrell didn't respond. Maybe he was already beyond earshot. More likely he saw no point in trading insults. Carter knew words were of little value, but as weapons, they drew no blood. And sometimes they stirred thought or transmitted wisdom. Both were in great need just then.

CHAPTER 11

FARRELL'S departure brought no peace. Carter had little appetite and barely touched his breakfast. He had no patience for the boys, and he was of little use working the stock. His mind was out past the river, in the rocks where Johnny was likely bleeding away his life. Brady had washed the blood from the saddle, but he hadn't erased it from Carter's memory.

"There's nothing you can do," Hope told him over and over. "Don't torture yourself. It was bound to happen."

"Maybe," Carter grumbled. The words brought no comfort, and toward dusk he rode up Antelope Mountain to share his news with Walt Harper.

"Gray Ghost, eh?" old Walt muttered. "Not a bad name. I'd bet he's far from dead. Johnny's got a tough hide, and Farrell's a braggart. I'll bet the boy's not half so bad hurt as you've been made to think."

"Even so, he's got no horse, and the whole county's on the alert. Look over there at those rocks. See my shadow?"

"I've had one of my own since daybreak," Walt replied. "Oh, yeah, Farrell's got his spies out. But Johnny's got a habit of blending into the night."

Carter wished he could share Walt Harper's optimism. The odds were too great, though. And Walt hadn't seen those scalped boys in the bed of Copeland's wagon.

Carter returned to the house as gloomy as ever. Dinner passed in an uneasy silence. The boys seemed afraid to speak. Even Richmond shrank from his father's gaze. Only little Rachel, her bright eyes flashing in the lamplight, babbled away to her father. Carter held the girl on his lap and tried to find peace. It failed to come, and when the others took to their beds, he again drifted through the house like the tormented soul he had become.

An hour after midnight Carter had his first hint that visitors had arrived. The horses in the corral whinnied nervously, and birds fluttered into higher branches. He took his shotgun and walked nervously outside. No stampeding hooves drew his attention. No howling mob of raiders descended. Instead, a slight figure darted toward the barn. Carter raced over and flung the shadowy intruder against the door.

"Move and you're dead!" Carter warned, touching the cold twin barrels of his shotgun to the bare back of the captive.

"I only came for horses," an anxious voice answered.

Carter immediately backed away, letting the faint light of a new moon dance across the face of Runs Long.

"Is this the way you come to me?" Carter asked. "Like a thief in the night? When did I ever refuse my own brother anything?"

"Was my idea," Johnny answered.

Carter turned and beheld Johnny's bent body. Owl Eyes supported him.

"Johnny?" Carter gasped, rushing over and easing his brother's heavy body to the ground. "Lord, they've shot you to pieces."

"I just came for horses," Johnny muttered. "We have to go."

"Look at yourself," Carter argued. "You can't go anyplace. Don't you know they're looking for you everywhere? Come on. Let's get you inside."

As Carter helped his brother along to the house, a lamp lit the front room. Soon J. T. rushed out to help. By the time Johnny was inside, the whole family was roused.

"It's a wonder you're not dead," Carter declared as he cut away his brother's shirt. A bullet had lodged in Johnny's left shoulder, and shots had shattered both legs. In addition, a gash had been torn across Johnny's chest, and a bullet had taken a shallow slice from his neck.

Someone had bound the wounds, but already there was festering. Carter and J. T. carried the half-dead figure to the kitchen table and stretched him out.

"I'll boil the water," Hope said, yawning away her weariness. "Brady, J. T., tear a sheet into bandages. You'd better fetch the medicine chest."

"You want me to cut the bullets out?" Carter asked.

"You?" Hope asked, chuckling. "You're as clumsy as an ox, and you don't have much stomach for blood. I'll do what needs doing. You see if you can find some spirits. He'll need something for the pain."

"Sure," Carter agreed.

He found a jug of corn liquor and poured three cups in turn. Johnny sipped each in turn. Before long he lost all feeling below the neck. Hope then took a deep breath and began cutting. The wounds bled freely, and she worked feverishly to extract the bullets before Johnny bled to death.

She removed all three with a gentle, patient touch. Carter admired her more than ever, knowing as he did that she had little stomach for blood herself. The wounds were seared with a hot knife, and Carter bound each tightly. Then Brady bathed his uncle's broken body and cleaned the table.

Hope, meanwhile, had a look at Runs Long and Owl Eyes. The elder of the boys was a bit bruised and battered but otherwise well. Scrubbed up and dressed in a shirt and trousers, Runs Long appeared none the worse for the ordeal.

Not so Owl Eyes. The boy was J. T.'s age, but the months of eluding cavalry and angry ranchers had left the young Indian thin and exhausted. At thirteen, he remained half a foot shy of matching J. T.'s five feet, and a heavy blow on the side of the face had closed one eye. Worse, a knife had slashed Owl Eye's left arm down to the bone. Hope drained the wound, then sewed the torn flesh together.

"Do you feel like riding?" she asked when J. T. brought a scrubbed Owl Eyes back to the kitchen.

"Hope?" Carter asked in surprise.

"They can't stay here," she said. "You know Farrell will be back. You'll never hide them from all the eyes that watch this place."

"I can take 'em to Walt's," Brady suggested.

"They're watching the cabin, too," Carter responded.

"There's good cover up there, though," Brady pointed out. "Caves, too. I'll bet I could hide there a year."

Carter turned toward the young Comanches. Owl Eyes shuddered, but Runs Long nodded.

"We have hidden before," the older refugee remarked. "There is good hunting there. We can survive."

"There's no moving Johnny," Carter warned.

"Not yet," she admitted. "We'll have to pray he mends fast. Otherwise we may all be on the run."

Carter knelt beside his brother's bandaged body. Johnny muttered half-coherent phrases. Whether the pain or the spirits had muddled his thinking wasn't certain. Clearly, though, the Gray Ghost would go nowhere for some time.

"Come on," Brady called to his cousins. "We'd better get along. It's a fair walk, and I have to be home before first light."

"Wait a minute," Hope called. She quickly filled a flour sack with what provisions could be spared, then kissed Brady on the forehead. "Take care," she urged.

"I will," Brady promised as he led the way outside.

Carter watched with pride how quickly the three young men blended into the shadows. They were gray ghosts themselves. Why not? Carter asked himself. It was a talent long nurtured.

With Brady off to Walt's, Carter returned to Johnny's side. With J. T.'s help, Hope had carried the wounded warrior to Brady's bed. Johnny moaned and tossed anxiously. His chest and head were burning with fever, and Hope brought a cool cloth. J. T. took it and began bathing his uncle's tortured face.

Carter shuddered. Already the bandages were growing red. Johnny's lifeblood was flowing out of him. A rag muffled his cries so as not to betray him to anyone observing from the surrounding hills.

"I don't know why he hasn't died," Hope announced. "He's in such pain, and there's nothing I can do."

"You did what was to be done," Carter declared. "The flesh will mend, and he'll grow stronger."

"How? He's bled near to death."

"Rosses are stubborn creatures, Hope. They don't give up so easy as some. Even as a little kid, Johnny was a fighter."

"Oh?" she asked, gripping his hand.

"I remember when he was just ten we had some Kiowas visit us. They'd been up in Kansas, and one of their children had come down with sickness. Our medicine man, Nighthawk's uncle, went to have a look. He came back with tales of a spotted sickness which burned like a council fire. It wasn't a week before the medicine man himself came down with it. Sickness raced through that camp like wildfire on the summer prairie."

"Smallpox?" J. T. asked. "I heard how it killed off lots of tribes up north."

"Measles," Carter explained. "Measles! I had 'em when I was six. Most everybody at the fort had 'em. We spent a few days in bed, then popped to our feet. It hit the Comanches hard, though. I'll bet near three quarters of the children in Nighthawk's camp died of it. Men and women, too. Swallow was feverish herself, and I tended Johnny. Nobody could understand why I didn't catch it. Nighthawk made prayers and fasted. Lots of the men danced and chanted. They built sweatlodges and smoked over it. Nothing worked."

"But Johnny survived."

"He fought it, Hope. He was little then, barely as big as Nate. I'd sit beside him and wipe his forehead like J. T.'s doing right now. I'd pray and whisper encouragement. Finally the fever broke, and he regained his strength."

"So your prayers were answered," she observed. "I guess God responds sometimes after all."

"Sure," Carter admitted. "He saved one skinny boy and carried off dozens of others. And he saved him for what—for some addled fool like Farrell to shoot him in the dead of night?"

"Saved him to help us through the war," she suggested. "To help see Nighthawk's boys raised. Maybe, once he grows well again, he'll realize there's a better path than raiding."

"You think he'll have a chance to choose?" Carter asked. "Will any of us? Do we ever?"

It certainly didn't seem so.

The remainder of that night Carter sat with Johnny. J. T. sank into the nearby bed, exhausted, and Hope returned to her room to try to find what little rest she could. Brady returned an hour before dawn. He stumbled without speaking to his room and lay in the blankets his mother had arranged on the floor.

At daybreak, Hope relieved Carter at the bedside, and he finally took to his bed. Exhaustion brought the first untroubled sleep in days, and he awoke to find half the morning gone.

"How's Johnny?" he asked Hope when he joined her in the kitchen.

"Better," she said. "The fever's broken. J. T.'s with him. They jabber at each other, but there's no sense to be made of it. Half the time Johnny speaks Spanish or Comanche. It's a muddle."

"He's likely out of his head."

"I hope so. He's apt to be in a lot of pain otherwise."

Carter nodded, then snatched a square of cornbread and nibbled on it. Nate and Rich brought in a bucket of water from the well, and Carter helped them fill the water barrel. Rachel sat in the far corner visiting with her new doll.

"Have you noticed if our friend's still watching?" Carter asked the boys.

"Moss Copeland's up there today," Nate answered. "He was down to get some water a while back. Asked if we'd had company."

"What did you tell him?" Carter asked nervously.

"Ma says we shouldn't lie," Nate said, hesitating. "But I don't guess it's lying exactly if you don't tell everything."

"So?" Carter asked.

"We told him some people came out yesterday and brought our horses back," Nate said, grinning. "Uncle Johnny's really not company anyway. He's family."

"You did just fine, son," Carter said.

"Ma says Uncle Johnny's invisible," Rich added. "Nobody else is supposed to know he's here."

"That's right," Carter agreed.

"Is he in trouble?" Nate asked.

"Not so long as we keep his secret," Carter replied. "There are men around who would harm him. We can't let that happen."

"We won't," Rich pledged.

Carter drew them close a minute, then left them to finish their chores as he looked in on Johnny.

"You look worn to the bone," Carter told J. T. "Think you can catch some sleep while I tend your patient?"

"I'm all right," J. T. said, shaking off his fatigue. "He's better, Pa. He wakes up sometimes and asks about his legs. They hurt pretty bad, I'd say."

"That's what comes of getting yourself shot."

"Pa, what'll happen if Hadley's pa and Jasper Farrell come back?"

Not if, Carter thought as he squeezed his son's weary shoulders. When.

"Pa?"

"I'll do my best to argue 'em away," Carter explained. "Once the bleeding stops and the wounds start to heal, we can hide Johnny in the cellar. For now, we just have to trust we'll have some time."

"I said a prayer for him," J. T. whispered. "I know you don't put much stock in such things, but I prayed you'd come back from Tennessee, and you did."

"It's important to believe in things, son. I guess my problem's always been that I'm at cross purposes with the Lord. I ask one thing, and He's determined to do something else."

"Yeah," J. T. said, grinning. "I do that, too. Reverend Hollings says it's a sinful thing to pray for selfish reasons, but why pray at all if you don't want something awful bad?"

Carter laughed and gripped the boy's shoulders. J. T. seemed to be growing daily of late, and summer had brought new muscle and a leathery feel to the youngster's tanned skin. If not for the yellow-white hair, J. T. could almost have been a second coming of Johnny Ross. Well, they did share a name.

Carter's attention was suddenly snatched by the sound of galloping hooves outside. Brady broke out of his slumber and pulled aside his blankets. J. T. tensed, and Johnny moaned.

"Close the curtains," Carter told Brady. "You boys stay here and see your uncle doesn't cry out. I'll see who's come calling."

"Be careful, Pa," J. T. urged.

Carter nodded. Their worried eyes made him cautious, and he buckled on his pistol before grabbing the shotgun. Outside, Carter waved Nate and Rich inside the house and turned to face Jasper Farrell, Ben Copeland, and three strangers.

"Mornin', Ross," Farrell called. "Fine day for workin' horses. You don't seem too busy, though."

"We've just been to Weatherford, you know," Carter explained. "You know the summer's a poor season for selling horses."

"Good time to trail cattle, though," Copeland commented.

"Lots of herds travelin' through. I sent word to Bob Bishop that I'd send four hands and two hundred steers with him to Dodge City. He might take your eldest boy along and some of your stock."

"Brady's just fourteen," Carter said, "and with all this trouble of late, I don't know that I'd care to have him on the trail."

"Well, I'm holdin' Hadley back for the same reason," Copeland confessed. "Bishop might still be agreeble to takin' on some steers, though. Give it some thought."

"I will," Carter said, scratching his head. "Isn't this a bit odd, you doing me favors?"

"Well," Copeland said, taking off his hat and wiping his brow, "Mary Elizabeth heard about us havin' words th' other day. She put me in mind of how you rode over and helped when those Comanches hit my place, and, well, I figured I might owe you."

"You don't."

"See?" Farrell remarked. "I told you he'd turn you down."

"I wouldn't judge that's what he said at all," Copeland barked. "Thing is, though, we'd all feel better about sendin' men north if these Comanches were rounded up."

"I thought you did that," Carter said. "You mean that ghost wasn't in the rocks after all?"

"These three fellows spied some Indians headin' along the river on foot," Copeland explained. "We trailed 'em a ways, then lost the tracks in the Brazos."

"They couldn't've up and disappeared," Farrell argued. "You seen 'em?"

"No," Carter declared.

"If you was to spot 'em, it'd put you in high regard with your neighbors," one of the strangers commented. "We hear you've got a halfbreed brother with those raiders."

"Oh?" Carter asked. "I *do* have a brother, and he's part Comanche, but I didn't know anybody identified him."

"When'd you last see him?" Farrell asked.

"It's been a while. Months."

"He knows more'n he says," Farrell growled. "Copeland, it's time we had a real search of this place."

"You that ready to die, Farrell?" Carter asked, cocking both hammers and raising the shotgun.

"You're awful nervous about havin' us look around," the last man in line pointed out. "Maybe you're hidin' those Comanches inside."

"Sure, I am," Carter said, grinning. "Quannah comes to tea once a week, and ole Lone Wolf's keeping him company today. Copeland, your boy Moss's been watching all morning, and before that, you had somebody else up there. You really think I'm stupid not to know that? Assuming I was to know these raiders or how to get word to 'em, would I bring anybody here?"

"Don't seem too likely," the man in back admitted. "We're wastin' our time here."

"I'd sure feel better if I was to take a look through that house," Farrell told his companions.

"Go ahead," Copeland said, laughing. " 'Course Ross there's apt to blow your carcass halfway to the river, but you're welcome to try."

Farrell frowned and led the others back toward Ioni Creek. Carter sighed and turned back to the house. Once inside, he removed the gunbelt and returned the shotgun to its high shelf over the door.

When Carter returned to Brady's and J. T.'s room, Johnny was sitting up.

"I seem to bring you only trouble and worry," he told Carter. "Wasn't my idea to come here."

"Where else would you go?" Carter asked. "This is home. As to trouble and worry, you've been doing that for as many years as I can remember. Brothers sometimes do."

"Soon I'll leave."

"Not for a long time," Carter said, pointing to the bandages. "You won't walk for weeks."

"What of Owl Eyes and Runs Long?"

"They're with old Walt," Brady explained. "I took 'em there myself."

"Then Walt's in danger, too," Johnny declared. "As you are. This Farrell has the dark eyes, Cart. He'll not rest till we're all dead. Or he is."

"He's a fool," Carter said sourly. "Nobody hereabouts pays him much mind."

"You should," Johnny said, sinking back onto his back. "I've seen his kind before. They kill too easily."

"Well, you're safe here," Carter told him. "You just let yourself mend. We'll worry about Jasper Farrell another day."

CHAPTER 12

IT was hard to forget about Jasper Farrell, though. He made daily visits to the ranch and questioned Carter's every action. Alone or with a company of companions, Farrell cast insults about with a recklessness that might have made a wiser man wary.

"Just lookin' for that Gray Ghost," Farrell always declared in parting.

Carter couldn't rid himself of the sensation that Farrell knew who the quarry was—and quite possibly where.

As the summer sun beat down mercilessly on the wild, dry Texas prairies, word came almost every week of some small band of Comanches struggling into Ft. Sill to take refuge at the reservation. One larger band, perhaps fifty strong, was surrounded by cavalry north of Ft. Griffin and escorted northward. Carter found it hard to listen as his neighbors celebrated such tidings.

"Soon no one will keep the old ways," Johnny lamented when Carter shared the news. "I think Nighthawk was the lucky one. For him the end came swiftly. I fear I'll be the last to ride the Llano."

"No one rides the Llano even now," Carter explained. "Farms and ranches are being staked out along the creeks and rivers. It's all over, Johnny."

"Not so long as I can walk."

"That's just it," Carter argued. "You *can't* walk."

Johnny dropped his head and sadly whistled a mournful tune.

"You always knew there was no chance of winning," Carter told him. "Now maybe you'll face facts."

"How strange it is to listen to you say those words," Johnny remarked, grinning soberly. "I hear you, but your heart's not speaking. You've known freedom, Cart. Could you live out your life in that jail of a reservation?"

"You wouldn't have to go there. You could stay here."

"You forget I'm not alone. What of Runs Long and Owl Eyes? What would they do?"

"Live," Carter said. "What will happen if you return to the Llano? In truth, it'd take a miracle to get you out of Palo Pinto County. Farrell's not forgotten. He hasn't given up the hunt."

But by August, most everyone else had. There remained talk of Gray Ghost, but dread had changed to mystery and awe. Even once bitter enemies like Ben Copeland spoke of the last Comanche raider and shared stories that the town boys soon spun into legends.

"Maybe peace has finally come," Hope whispered as she and Carter walked along the creek one twilight around the middle of the month. "Lord knows we're entitled."

It seemed true, too. The watch on the hillside had been abandoned, and the hardest stares of townfolk had begun to soften. J. T. and Brady were often invited to share their afternoons with Hadley and Moss Copeland, and their father did indeed arrange for 200 Ross steers to be driven north to the Kansas railheads.

But as always whenever a hint of brightness appeared on the horizon, an ill wind swept it away. Jasper Farrell was behind it. The sometime rancher, former scout, and relentless Indian hater arrived with two dusty ex–buffalo hunters.

"I guess you're surprised to see me, eh?" Farrell asked.

"Oh, I don't know," Carter said, shaking his head. "August is hot, and it tends to drive snakes up out of the rocks."

"Not Comanches, though," Farrell grumbled. "Been awful quiet for summer."

"Cavalry's been rounding up what's left of the Comanches, or so I hear," Carter explained. "With new settlements springing up to the west, any Comanche would have to be a ghost to stay in the open for long."

"Maybe. Most folks, includin' our friend Copeland, say that Gray Ghost is dead. Nowadays, half a dozen men claim to've killed him down in the rocks. But how can you kill somethin' you can't see? Answer that, will you? We found no body, and a man, livin' or dead, has got flesh and bones. I've been through that country upriver inch by inch, and I've found nothin'. He's not there, Ross, so he's not dead."

"Maybe he was one of the ones the cavalry dragged in."

"I rode up to the reservation and asked around. Those Indians up there are worn out, used up. They told me this and that, but none of 'em rode with Gray Ghost."

"None admitted it, you mean," Carter said, grinning. "I can see why not. They'd hardly be willing to stick their neck in a noose. A man was killed at the Copeland place, wasn't he?"

"Oh, they wouldn't have to worry about that sort of judgment. In truth, we'd never take the trouble to drag some buck down here for trial. We evened up that score long ago."

"Why don't you just forget about that Indian," Carter suggested. "If he's not dead, he's certainly fled the area."

"I don't think so," Farrell declared. "I'd bet my life he's still hereabouts. You could find him."

"I wouldn't bank on that. If he's as clever as you say, he's too tricky for me to track."

"I'll pay some Tonkawas to track," Farrell explained. "I need you to go up to Ft. Sill with me, talk to some of the ones who've just come in from the Llano. They can tell you lots, and you can tell me."

"Why should I?"

"The man who brings in Gray Ghost will be a man long remembered around here, Ross. I aim to be that man, but I'll share the glory with you. And there's close to a thousand dollars reward offered by some Young County ranchers."

"I don't need the money," Carter declared. "I've got more

work than I can get to as it is without setting out on some ghost hunt."

"This one would prove profitable," Farrell argued. "People haven't forgotten you refused to ride with us after Copeland's place was hit. They'd take note of your help now. Sooner or later, you'll come along. You have to decide who you are. Are you red or white? May come a time when you need friends and neighbors. As it is, you're not makin' many. Who'd lift a finger to help a man that hid Indians?"

"What?"

"Well, I can't be sure you actually hid any of 'em, but I'm certain you've done your best to keep us from findin' 'em."

"I've done what I always do," Carter said angrily. "Mind my own business. Some would do well to profit from my example. As for needing friends, I've always thought it best to rely on my own self. I get a lot less disappointment that way, Farrell!"

"I'll find that Comanche," Farrell promised. "You just hope to heaven I don't find him anywhere near your property. There'll be a day of reckoning, Ross. You can bank on it."

Farrell then led the others westward, and Carter slowly made his way to the house.

"He won't let go of the scent, not even when the trail's gone ice cold," Carter grumbled. "He's dangerous, that Farrell. He doesn't know everything, but he's close enough to the truth to cause us trouble."

"Maybe," Johnny admitted. "But a hunter must use caution, Carter. Otherwise he may find himself the prey."

Carter frowned. He didn't care to think of Johnny returning to the Llano, but he truly dreaded the notion of his brother resuming the raids. Of course, neither would happen anytime soon. Johnny could walk only with the aid of crutches carved from willow limbs. The sticks were troublesome at best, but legs shot to pieces didn't heal overnight.

Owl Eyes, on the other hand, seemed to grow stronger with the passing of each day. Together with Runs Long, the boys would visit the ranch under the cloak of darkness. No sentries watched Walt's place now either, but the prospect of blundering across some idle rider kept the boys cautious.

"You can hardly tell where the knife cut," Carter said, observing Hope's handiwork as he turned Owl Eyes's arm from side to side. The stitching formed only a slight indentation now. Old Walt knew how to nurse wounds, and perhaps Johnny, too, might have done better under the watchful eyes and constant attention of the old soldier. Carter never voiced such opinions aloud, of course. Hope would have declared it just so much nonsense and charged them as ungrateful.

It was a joy to watch Johnny's spirits return. He brightened considerably whenever the boys were around. Often he would send Owl Eyes and Runs Long out to gather some berries or dig a particular root. Then, with arms painted appropriately, Johnny would summon Brady, J. T., Nathan, and Richmond. In the pitch black of the lampless room, Johnny would share some tale of the old times. If it wasn't too frightening and she hadn't already taken to her bed, Rachel would join them. Carter and Hope kept clear, though.

"He's at his best with the children," Hope observed.

"Sometimes I think it's what he knows best," Carter told her. "He's spent half his life looking after somebody. Being the youngest, he should have been free of that. But first came the war. I went away, and he stood in my place. Then when I came home, the cavalry made war on Nighthawk and the rest of the Kwahadis. There were always boys without fathers from then on, and being one himself, I suppose Johnny's heart went out to them."

"It seems strange to me that such a gentle man should be called upon to lead others in war."

"I know," Carter agreed. "But no one chooses his life. I never wanted to ride east. Lord knows the times I wished to escape the cold or the heat, the killing and the dying. It passed, though, and I came home. War's in Johnny's past, too, now."

"Is it past?" she asked. "I heard what Jasper Farrell said, and I see what's in Johnny's eyes."

"Give it time."

"Time?" she whispered. "I've never known a place to hurry life like the frontier, Carter. It turns small boys into field hands. When they're still fuzzy-cheeked and full of wonderment like Brady, something grabs them and makes them hard. I read that hardness in Hadley Copeland. I see traces of it in Brady. I pray for time, Carter, but deep down I know it's the enemy."

He held her tightly. And later, when Johnny had spun his final tale, and the young Comanches had departed for the safety of Walt's cabin, Carter spoke to his brother.

"Who can tell what tomorrow will bring?" Johnny asked, resting on his crutches. "Maybe the President will read the Medicine Lodge Treaty and give us back our home. Maybe Jasper Farrell will fall down a well."

"Maybe Johnny Ross will put aside his gun and help me raise horses. And kids."

"It sounds so easy," Johnny said, sighing. "It isn't. We are the last of the old times, Cart. We remember the buffalo. We rode with Nighthawk, hunted and fished and roped the wild stallions of the hills. Is it possible to forget? Is it possible to live inside walls and shut out the song of the earth and the face of the sky?"

"I've done that a long time now, little brother."

"Maybe it's the blood of your white mother. My blood burns with the old ways. So it is with Owl Eyes and Runs Long."

"The old ways will only lead to an early grave for all of you," Carter argued. "It's finished. The task at hand is to find a door to the new world without losing yourself entirely."

"You've tried," Johnny said, gazing intently into his brother's eyes. "What has it brought you? You led their young men in war. You bled for them. You came back with the stars of a colonel on your coat, but they gave you no honor. These people only remembered you lived in an Indian camp as a boy, that your father wed a Comanche."

"They don't understand."

"They don't?" Johnny asked. "I don't. I've watched soldiers ride to our camp and call for talk. Then while our people prepare the pipe, the bluecoats ride down our women and children, burn our lodges, and shoot our ponies. There's no understanding such madness. The world cries out in sadness. I've ridden with the Cheyenne. They were sent to the reservation, Carter. It's a place where people go to die. If my life has to be short, I will live it in the old way, and I will die a free man."

"Johnny, there's no good way to die."

"You're wrong. All the choices a man has lead to death in the end. It's always better to die standing tall, facing the enemy. Too many have been shot in their sleep, swallowed by cold and silent death. I won't go quietly, Cart. I'll fight 'em long and hard."

"Fight who?" Carter asked. "I've seen the face of war, too, you know. For three years we rode across Tennessee, besting the enemy near every time. Those last months we all knew it was hopeless, but it was easier to keep fighting than to accept defeat. Half my regiment fell during that time. A lot of 'em just gave up and threw their lives away. Johnny, I've only got one brother, and I don't plan to build him a scaffold on Antelope Mountain."

Johnny gazed at his feet, and Carter helped him back to the room he shared with Brady and J. T.

"It's a fool speaks of death too often," Johnny said as Carter helped him to the bed.

"Yes," Carter agreed. And he hoped somehow that peace might last a little longer, long enough perhaps to find a way to keep death at bay.

CHAPTER 13

PEACE was, at best, elusive. Too often it vanished in the blink of an eye, so Carter wasn't surprised when Hadley Copeland brought word of new trouble.

"Our stock's been raided," the fifteen-year-old announced. "Pa said to spread the word. Could be they came through this way."

"No," Carter said, shaking his head. "You're the first one to come by in a couple of days. You've lost stock, you say? How many?"

"Thirty, forty head, I'd guess."

"Rustlers," Carter grumbled. "We had some trouble with 'em before the war. I'd say they drove your animals north, up to Buffalo Springs or even to the Nations. That or back east to Jacksboro. Nobody down south or west would buy your brand. It's too well known."

"Indians wouldn't take 'em to sell," Hadley declared. "They'd live all winter off a small herd."

"Comanches?" Carter asked. "I never knew 'em to tie themselves to that much livestock. Sure, they've taken an animal or two. Most times they slaughter 'em right away and pack the meat."

"Well, you'd know more 'bout that than me, Mr. Ross. I only came to pass on the word. Pa'll be by afterwhile himself. He's gone to talk to Jasper Farrell."

"Sure," Carter said, frowning as Hadley turned back toward Ioni Creek and hurried south to spread the news. So, once again trouble was afoot. And if Farrell was involved, no good would come of it.

Carter met briefly with Ben Copeland two hours later.

"It appears I'm havin' a run of bad luck," Copeland grumbled. "First those Comanches burn my barn. Now they run off my stock."

"I can't see Indians behind this," Carter argued.

"Hadley told me your feelings, but a couple of young bucks were spotted out this way last week."

"Near here?" Carter asked. "Nonsense. Even if there were a couple of stragglers hereabouts, they could hardly herd thirty head on foot. If they'd ridden horses, I would have picked up their sign."

"There's plenty of sign," Copeland declared. "I'll show you."

Carter mounted a horse and followed his neighbor to the Copeland ranch. Along the river, tracks of five or six horses appeared in the sand. Carter dismounted and examined the tracks carefully.

"Shod horses," Carter pointed out. "Not Indian ponies."

"Ross, half the outfits along the river have lost saddle horses to those Indians," Copeland reminded Carter. "I wouldn't think that much of a sign."

"Oh? Then think about this. The trail shows four, maybe five horsemen were here. Tell me how they'll eat thirty head of cattle before winter's through?"

"The rest of their band's probably hiding somewhere close."

"Just waiting for you to ride down on 'em? All you'd have to do is follow the cattle trail."

"Indians move fast."

"Without horses, trailing cattle? Or maybe they're riding your steers."

"They could sell the cattle or swap 'em for horses."

"Could they?" Carter asked. "Would you buy branded cattle from a Comanche? Most places around here an Indian gets shot on sight. No, what I told your boy's more likely. Rustlers ran your stock up to Buffalo Springs or maybe Jacksboro. Look for 'em there."

"We could use help followin' this trail," Copeland said, gazing northward. "You know the land, and you're a fine tracker. Everyone says so."

"They also call me a Comanche half-breed behind my back. No, Copeland, the trail's easily followed, and you've got seven or eight men riding for you. I'm needed at home. Besides, I have no stomach for hunting other men anymore."

"Nor for huntin' justice?"

"I don't always have the same notion of what justice is that most folks around here have. It's been a long time since anybody spoke of a trial or fetching a sheriff."

Copeland frowned. The words had struck home.

"You're right," Copeland admitted. "But it takes forever to get the sheriff out this way, and he wouldn't ride north with us. Besides, this is kind of personal."

"Sure," Carter said, nodding his understanding. "You got to see that I've got no stake in it, though."

"I do," Copeland replied. "I thank you for comin' out here and takin' a look. While I'm gone, I'd consider it a kindness if you'd keep your eye on Ioni Creek and your ear to the wind."

"I'll see your family's not bothered."

Copeland nodded in acknowledgement of the favor. Carter mounted his horse and headed homeward.

As it happened, Copeland had a dozen men in the saddle early the next morning. They followed Jasper Farrell northward. For the first time in what seemed like ages, no neighbor's eyes scouted Ross's Gap, and Carter found himself enjoying those final days of summer.

When not working the stock or tending to chores, Carter would usher the boys down to Ioni Creek. They'd devote an hour or so to splashing away their weariness or snagging catfish. Owl Eyes and Runs Long would sometimes join in the fun, and as Johnny's legs began to strengthen, he would appear as well. For the briefest of times Carter felt the hands on the clock had frozen. The boys were six of a kind just then. Bronze-skinned Owl Eyes and white-haired J. T. might resemble each other about as much as a pea does a carrot, but their laughter and antics brought out a kinship shared by all boys their fourteenth summer.

The boys rekindled the sparkle in Johnny's eyes.

"Perhaps the world isn't so crazy as I thought," Johnny observed. "They aren't so different from you and me, Carter."

"They will be," Carter said sadly. "There are no buffalo to hunt. Soon there'll be no mustangs to chase down."

"The creeks will flow," Johnny said, grinning as Brady captured little Nate in his arms and dragged the younger boy into midstream. The both of them howled and splashed wildly. "A man can grow strong and swift on venison," Johnny added. "So long as he doesn't lose the old ways."

Carter thought to announce the old ways dead and buried, but little Owl Eyes produced a flute and blew a long-forgotten tune. The boy's shining eyes and bright laughter were so much like Swallow, the aunt Owl Eyes had never known.

Perhaps the old ways do live on, Carter thought. Some part of that gentle woman should survive. And as he shared tales of better times and remembered a childhood too swiftly spent, Carter hoped Brady and J. T., Nate and Rich would hold those stories close. They were an anchor against a sea of change sweeping in from all around them.

The final week of August, Carter urged more caution. Ben Copeland and his companions had recaptured most of the stolen stock, but the rustlers remained at large. Again Jasper Farrell prowled the county, and it was no longer safe for Johnny, Owl Eyes, or Runs Long to splash away an afternoon at Ioni Creek.

Johnny remained at the house, impatiently waiting for his legs to mend. For safety, he had moved to the cellar, though. Walt, eager to lift the spirits of his two young companions, set off on a deer hunt. Runs Long appeared at the house three days later with word that a buck and a doe had been shot.

"Walt says you should come for supper," Runs Long explained. "We'll smoke the pipe and dance. The meat of the deer will make our legs swift once more."

Johnny looked at his bent left leg, and Carter scowled. That leg would never again run. But when they gathered at the barn to mount horses for the ride to Antelope Mountain, Johnny discarded his sticks.

"Time to mend," Johnny declared, tossing the crutches aside. "I stand on my own legs from now on."

Carter watched his brother wince at each step taken, but there was little choice. Recovery never came unless the price was paid in pain. And Johnny did seem to grow less lame. Or perhaps he had only conquered the pain.

One way or the other, it cheered Runs Long to see Johnny mounted. The young Comanche was equally glad to climb atop a pinto pony himself. Carter, meanwhile, got the children mounted. He passed little Rachel up to Brady. Rich climbed up behind J. T. Now that Nathan was eight, he would ride alone. Hope sat atop a chestnut mare between her eldest sons. Carter climbed onto a big gray and waved the others to follow Runs Long and Johnny.

They headed up the time-worn path to Walt's cabin, then continued along the rocky ridge into a clearing surrounded by scrub junipers and sprinkled liberally with prickly pear and pencil cactus. A bed of coals occupied the center of the clearing. Owl Eyes tended strips of cooking venison there.

" 'Bout time you folks happened along," old Walt called from the far end of the fire. He was stirring a kettle and overseeing batches of cornbread baking in a Dutch oven.

"Can't expect us to be eager if you've had a hand in the cooking, Walt," Carter replied, laughing. "You like to starve Johnny and me growing up. A plate of boiled skunk in Nighthawk's camp was a feast compared to your old squirrel stews."

"Don't you believe it, youngsters," Walt growled. "Those two would lick my stirring spoon clean, not to mention their bowls. They grew fat on my grub."

"Fat?" J. T. asked with raised eyebrows. "Pa and Uncle Johnny were fat?"

"Well, fat compared to a bowstring," Johnny said, masking the pain of dismounting by laughing loudly.

At the urging of the children, Hope set off to have a look at the cornbread, and Carter gave Owl Eyes a hand with the meat. Soon all was ready for a feast, and Walt spread some ancient blankets beside the fire. Rachel nestled in between her mother and father. Walt and Owl Eyes served food, and Johnny spread the boys in a half-circle around the blankets.

Runs Long then made prayers to the deer and prepared the pipe. Rachel fidgeted a bit, and Richmond whispered questions. Both grew quiet, though, as Johnny accepted the pipe and puffed it ceremoniously.

"I thank the spirits for bringing us all together this night," Johnny called to the sky overhead. "To the deer, who give us swift legs to carry us, we are grateful, too."

Johnny then added the other words, Comanche phrases that his little niece and nephews could not understand. There was a solemnity to the speech, though, and Carter smiled with satisfaction at the quiet reverence shared by the children.

Carter Ross knew those words, of course. They were a plea for health, for protection from that greatest and most heartless of enemies—time. Silently Carter prayed for the same. After all, Johnny was still safe, so perhaps God had taken rare pity on the Rosses.

The pipe made its way around their little circle. Walt puffed it and blessed the gathering. Brady puffed and close to choked on the smoke. J. T. was more cautious and barely touched the pipe to his lips. Runs Long sang softly, then spoke of the father and brother he wished were there beside him.

"Grant us understanding . . . and peace," Carter said when his turn came.

Owl Eyes took the pipe last, for Hope deemed Nate too young. The bright-eyed youngster spoke of the long and trying winter and the violent spring before chanting an ancient song.

"Make us strong, Man Above," Owl Eyes prayed. "Give us power to see our path and wisdom to take it."

Carter marveled at the depth of Owl Eyes's thoughts. If Nighthawk had lived, the boy would surely have been taught the medicine herbs and healing rituals. But even as Owl Eyes chanted again, Carter sensed a darkness falling across the boy's face. He returned the pipe to Runs Long, and Walt declared it time to eat. In no time, squares of cornbread, strips of venison, and spoonfuls of beans were gobbled down by eager diners. Afterward, Owl Eyes took out his flute, and Runs Long led the dancing.

Carter sat with Johnny as the boys tried to match Runs Long's wild movements. Even Rachel tried to hop along.

"This I miss most of all," Johnny whispered. "It will be a long time before I dance again."

"I wish there was a maiden here for you to court," Carter added. "I'd wish you the same happiness I've found with Hope."

"It's difficult for a man from two worlds to find a wife in either," Johnny explained. "I have my sons. Soon I may be glad not to have a woman to worry over."

"Loneliness isn't much of a substitute."

"No, but this is a bad time to take a woman, to give birth to little ones. There's a smell of death on the wind."

"I don't smell it," Carter objected. "Autumn's still got its full run to go, and we've got music to listen to and tales to spin for the children."

"Yes," Johnny agreed. but the same sadness that flowed across Owl Eyes's face took possession of Johnny's eyes. Carter tried to erase it from his own mind. Maybe it was a reaction to the joy and love shared by little Rachel and the boys, the closeness shared by Carter and Hope. Maybe it was knowing no such home was possible for a young Comanche. Perhaps Owl Eyes had the gift of dreams and could see the future.

Carter hoped not. A boy of thirteen should be too full of the great mystery. He should dance and run and laugh. Owl Eyes played his mournful flute and gazed sadly down the mountainside.

Lord, watch over them, Carter prayed again, stronger, with all the fervor he'd practiced as the five-year-old son of a Methodist preacher's daughter. If his mother had lived longer, Carter Ross might have been another Reverend Hollings, all full of self-assured piety, with answers for every question. Or perhaps not. Texas had a way of shaking the certainties out of a man. Given time, even Hollings might come to admit the world held out some mystery.

They returned to the house well past midnight. Carter carried Rachel and Richmond to their beds, and he had to provide some help to Nathan. J. T. and Brady helped their uncle down to the cellar. The day had been a long one, and it had taken a toll on Johnny's legs.

"I'm glad the boys had this night with Owl Eyes and Runs Long," Hope said when Carter joined her on the edge of their bed. "They'll remember this when they're older. You can explain the meaning of the ceremonies, and they'll be able to understand more about who they are."

"They're going to have a hard time," Carter said, sighing as she leaned her head on his shoulder and tenderly stroked his chest. "The world's changing so fast, and the old ways are slipping away."

"That's why I think Brady and J. T. should go to school in town," she whispered. "I agree Nate should stay at the ranch. I can teach him his figures and listen to him read. The others should go, though. Reverend Hollings says they've hired a real teacher this year, a widow from Waco. She's brought all sorts of books and maps. Carter, we owe our boys the same chance to understand the new world as they have to know the old one."

"You're right," he said, surrendering. "It's proper they should go. I admit I'm not pleased by it, and I'll not enjoy seeing 'em leave each morning and return late. I'll miss their efforts with the work, too."

"And I'll miss their company," Hope said, kissing his forehead. "The tough thing about being a mother is doing what's right for your kids, isn't it?"

"I've never been a mother."

"A father then."

"Yes," Carter agreed. "The real tough part's going to come when they return hurt or insulted, when they want to go to war against half the town because people call us names or doubt our word."

"Maybe that won't happen."

"Sure," Carter mumbled.

But that very next week when Brady and J. T. began attending the classes conducted by the new schoolmarm, Mrs. Ada Gill, trouble began. J. T. returned the second day bruised and battered. Brady was bitter but tight-lipped.

"I don't want to disappoint Ma," J. T. told Carter, "but except for Hadley and Moss, those other kids all hate us. They call us names and give us trouble. Pa, if I had a knife, I'd kill Si Porterfield and a couple of others."

"You can't do that," Carter said, placing his hands on J. T.'s shoulders and steadying the boy.

"Then I'm staying right here from now on," J. T. replied.

"You can't do that either, son. One thing I've learned painfully in this life is that you can never back down when the enemy thinks he's got you on the run. You have to hit back."

"I'd make a better impression with a knife."

"Not with your fists," Carter explained. "You strike back with your head. Show 'em how clever you are. Take their words and fire 'em back, twisted so they don't like their sound."

"I'll try, Pa," J. T. promised. "But if it doesn't get better, I'll head up Antelope Mountain and join Owl Eyes and Runs Long."

Carter grinned, and J. T. brightened, too. And though the problems in town continued, J. T. kept at his lessons and fought his battles with new and better words.

Hope grew more discouraged, though. Brady had turned downright gloomy, and the younger children had become more difficult to handle. They missed their older brothers, and Nate in particular squawked about being made to stay at home with the babies.

"I just don't know what to do, Carter," Hope told him. "Maybe it was a mistake to send them. The house is upside down, it seems."

"The whole world's upside down," Carter declared. "Don't let it shake you."

"The worst part is that I miss them, too."

"That comes of their growing up. Bound to happen. You know, I was riding to the buffalo hunt with Nighthawk when I was Brady's age. In a few years they'll be off starting their own families."

"I wish we could slow down time."

Me, too, Carter thought.

Brady and J. T. were not the only ones to venture forth from the ranch, either. Johnny had finally begin to walk normally. He confronted Carter with the news that it was time to leave.

"We've been too long under roofs and wearing white man's clothes," Johnny grumbled. "It's time we rode back to the Llano."

"Have you forgotten winter's coming?"

"Oh, there's time yet. Runs Long found a band of our people not so far from here. It's best we join them."

"You're with your people now."

"This is your house, your land, and your way, Cart," Johnny explained. "I make a bad white man. Sometimes I think you are not so good yourself. You were wise to send the boys to town. Brady will learn. J. T. has the blood of the old ones, though. Too much of you, too. He will have a hard path."

"Yes, I'm afraid he will."

"Now I must go. My path isn't easy, you see."

"Johnny, I so wish you'd stay. Things are settling down."

"It won't stay that way. Cart, Owl Eyes has dreams. He sees a bad time coming."

"All the more reason to stay. This is your home."

"No longer," Johnny said, gripping Carter's wrists. "Runs Long and Owl Eyes could never be at home here. They hunger for the midnight stars. I'm their father now, Cart. I must lead them. Perhaps after we've joined the others, we'll all go north into the mountains. The Cheyenne hunt the buffalo there, I've heard. Some of them have joined the Sioux. They still live free."

"Not for long. There are soldiers headed up there, too. Gold's been found in the Black Hills, it's said, and a gold rush will trample an Indian treaty to dust each and every time."

"Yes," Johnny said sadly. "But I must try just the same."

"You'll wait till tomorrow morning. That way you can say your good-byes to Rachel and the boys."

"Yes, and then I will ride."

Carter nodded sadly. A chill gripped his belly, and he couldn't help recalling the sad expression on Owl Eyes's face. Carter feared another long winter, and a spring of great despair.

CHAPTER 14

TWO mornings after Johnny's departure, Carter was overseeing morning chores when he sniffed an odd odor in the air. Brady noticed it, too, and set aside his water buckets. J. T. and Nate, tossing feed to the chickens ten feet away, shouted anxiously and pointed toward the south.

"Lord," Carter cried, staring at a dark line of twisting smoke rising skyward from the slope of Antelope Mountain. "Walt!"

Instantly J. T. and Brady hurried to the barn and fetched saddles. Carter raced inside the house and took a Winchester rifle from the gun rack. He loaded fresh shells in the gun's magazine as outside the boys readied horses.

"Carter?" Hope asked, reading the anxiety etched across his forehead.

"There's a fire at Walt's," Carter explained. "Could be trouble."

"Get help," she urged.

"Where?" Carter asked, making a slow turn around the room before stepping to the door. "Who'd help us?"

"At least take the boys," she urged.

J. T. and Brady were already mounted. Their father's horse pranced nervously between them.

"This won't be any swim in the creek," Carter told her. "Somebody could get hurt."

"I know," she said, shooing Rachel inside as she followed Carter to the horses. "All the more reason to take them with you."

Nate and Rich looked nervously up into their father's grave eyes. Carter gave each a reassuring nod, then stepped to the horse and slid the Winchester into a scabbard stitched to the side of the saddle. He didn't want the boys, any of them, along. There were too many uncertainties, too many dangers.

Carter glanced back at Hope. I know what she's thinking, he told himself. If they're along, I'll be cautious. But caution rarely held death at bay.

"All right," Carter reluctantly agreed as he climbed into the saddle. "You boys stay behind me, and don't even twitch if I don't say to do so."

Brady and J. T. nodded, and Carter turned to Nate and Rich.

"Look after your ma, Nate. You boys mind her, don't boss your sister too much, and finish the chores. Understand?"

"Yes, sir," they spoke as one.

Carter turned his horse and led the way toward Antelope Mountain. His eyes followed the smoke, and a sudden urgency filled every inch of his being. He raced across the open ground toward the mountain. Only when he started into the rocks did he slow the pace. Now he examined evey inch of the terrain before moving onward.

About a mile from Walt's cabin, the scent of charred timber grew stronger. Suddenly a line of riders sprang from out of the nearby junipers, and Carter pulled his rifle and steadied his horse.

"Hold there!" Carter called. The riders turned and broke down the slope of the mountain. All but one, that is. Jasper Farrell turned back toward Carter and waved a rifle in the air. Farrell's words were swallowed by the rapid pounding of hooves on the rocky trail nearby, but the fiery hatred in the man's eyes left little in doubt. Carter urged his horse along in a rapid trot, and soon he reached the smoldering ruin of the cabin.

"Walt!" Carter shouted. "Walt!"

There was no answer, and Carter tumbled off the side of the horse and surveyed the shambles of Walt's home. The barn was already in danger from spreading flames, and the house was clearly lost. Clothing and dry goods were strewn everywhere. A cyclone couldn't have done a better job of scattering a lifetime's accumulated belongings. Carter stood frozen in his tracks.

"Pa, we've got to get the fire put out," Brady cried. "It'll spread like mad once it hits the tall grass."

The urgency in Brady's words moved Carter to action. He waved the boys toward the well, then trotted to the barn and drew out four or five saddle blankets. Soon they were slapping the wet blankets against the spreading flames. An hour of choking, blinding labor halted the blaze. The remnant of the cabin continued to burn itself out, but there remained little danger of the flames spreading elsewhere.

Carter led his smoke-blackened sons back to the well. They doused themselves with water and coughed the smoke from their lungs. Then they fell, exhausted, to the ground.

"Who could've done such a thing?" J. T. asked.

"We saw 'em," Brady answered angrily. "Was Farrell."

"Why?" J. T. asked.

Brady turned to his father, and Carter frowned.

"Men like Farrell are full of a bitterness that eats out their insides, son," Carter explained. "They can never let their anger die. They feed it every chance they get, and they strike out without thinking."

J. T. frowned and walked off into the trees. The boy's emotions had a way of overwhelming him, and J. T. was reluctant to share such times. But no sooner did he vanish into the junipers than he cried out in anguish.

"Pa! Pa!"

Carter scrambled to his feet and raced to his son's side. J. T. plunged his tear-streaked face into his father's chest and sobbed. Carter steadied the boy. He gazed first at the terror in J. T.'s eyes and then behind the boy at what had put it there.

"Lord, no," Carter muttered, holding J. T. tightly and

stepping away from the two corpses at their feet. Old Walt lay nearest, his shirt torn away and an ugly T cut into his chest. The old man's lifeless eyes remained hauntingly fixed in an angry stare.

Beside Walt Harper lay Runs Long. The fifteen-year-old had been bared and scalped. His feet were badly burned, and his arms and chest were bruised.

"He was a long time dying," a solemn voice spoke from behind them. Carter jumped and quickly stepped in front of J. T. as if to shield the boy from any danger. The sad-faced speaker stepped from cover, though, extending his empty hands in a gesture of helplessness.

"Johnny?" Carter asked.

"I wasn't here when they came," Johnny explained, rubbing his eyes dry. "There was no need to do this. To kill is bad enough, but to cut letters into old men and scalp boys."

"It's for traitor," Brady declared, kneeling beside the bodies. "I heard Hadley's pa tell how they used to brand deserters during the war."

"What would he know of the war?" Carter asked angrily. "He never served the colors. Old Walt fought with Winfield Scott, chased Santa Anna out of Mexico City, fought more often and more places than he cared to speak of."

"It's a message," Johnny said, frowning. "For you."

"Or for you," Carter grumbled. "They'll know you're here."

"No, they know nothing," Johnny declared. "Runs Long never talked except to scream his pain and yell his curses. Look at him! He's but a boy still, and they did this to him!"

"He rode a warrior's trail," Carter whispered, helping his brother down the hillside. "I'll put him in a blanket, and the boys can cut scaffold poles. I'd like to bury Walt beside Pa back on the hill above Ioni Creek."

"I'll kill 'em for what they've done!" Johnny raged.

"What purpose will that serve?" Carter asked. "More blood? I'm sick of it! How many nightmares will I have to chase from Brady and J. T.? Will I wind up burying you, too? And what of Owl Eyes?"

"He saw it all in his dreams," Johnny explained, trembling like a leaf in the autumn breeze.

"And what else has he seen?"

"That they won't be the last."

"Lord, Johnny, don't do this."

"What else can I do? This is my blood that has flowed here. Nighthawk was a father to us. Was Walt any less one? It was my burden he carried today. I will avenge him."

"Vengeance? If you killed a hundred ranchers, Runs Long would still be dead. Johnny, it has to stop."

"It will," he promised. "Soon. There must be blood because of this, Carter. To kill in war I can forgive. But to burn and cut and scalp! I will find this Farrell and show him what it means to feel pain."

"There's other business at hand," Carter reminded his brother. "You will mourn the dead?"

"Yes," Johnny agreed. "I will honor them four days. Then I will avenge them."

Carter frowned. He then sent the boys to cut poles. He washed the bodies himself and wrapped them in the smoky saddle blankets. After taking Walt to the small plot above Ioni Creek and laying him in a grave beside Charleston Ross, he led the boys and Johnny to the cliff where Nighthawk and Buffalo Hump rested on scaffolds.

Owl Eyes was waiting for them. The boy chanted and played his flute. He placed his own bow and clothes upon Runs Long's platform.

"I cannot send my brother naked into the spirit places," Owl Eyes explained.

Johnny then joined the chant, and Carter drew his sons close. Not so long ago Brady and J. T. had raced ponies with Runs Long and Buffalo Hump. They were only boys. To die so young was a terrible waste. To be scalped and tortured by the likes of Jasper Farrell was a crime against nature. Carter was half of a mind to join Johnny's revenge.

"I'm all that's left of my father," Owl Eyes spoke when the chanting seized. "Now I am the nighthawk. I will remember long."

Carter frowned as the boy's face grew cold and hard as stone. There was none of Nighthawk's gentle laughter now. It had been cut away, and now the boy's soul stood bare and bleeding.

They sadly rode through the gap in the mountains to Ioni Creek. There, with Hope and the little ones alongside, Carter and his brother bade Walt Harper a final farewell. Hope suggested asking for Reverend Hollings to ride out and read scripture over the grave on Sunday after services, but Carter considered the real memorial gathering right then. Johnny and Owl Eyes chanted, and Carter shared recollections of the old man who had been more of a father than Charleston Ross to sons that suddenly seemed far different than ever before.

When all the words that wanted saying were spoken, and all the feelings were shared, Hope led the children back to the house. Carter gripped his brother's wrists and said farewell.

"This will be the final time I'll come here," Johnny said, gazing westward. "It isn't safe for you . . . for the little ones. So I will ride far away."

Carter shuddered at the thought of Johnny and Owl Eyes fighting off a dozen horsemen.

"No," Carter pleaded. "Go to the reservation if you don't feel you can stay here. You can't last out there all alone, Johnny. You'll end up dead—like Nighthawk and old Walt. You're all the family I have left."

"No, you have sons. They'll grow tall at your side."

"You'll be all alone."

"Not for long. Owl Eyes had another dream. Others will

come to follow me. Young men from the reservation and others who have never left the plains."

"It will be a hard trail," Carter warned.

"It always has been," Johnny answered, leading Owl Eyes off across the creek and into the distant unknown.

Less than an hour later Jasper Farrell arrived at Ross's Gap. Carter could barely control his rage as the ex-scout shouted for Nate to clear the trail. The boy was laden with slop for the hogs and was nearly trampled.

"Don't you ever shout at that boy again, Farrell!" Carter shouted. His eyes blazed furiously, and for once Farrell was without words.

"I didn't . . . I didn't see . . . the boy till . . . I was on top of him," Farrell stammered. "I didn't come to mince words, Ross. I crossed a trail up at Walt Harper's place. It led me here."

"You saw me up there," Carter reminded Farrell. "I saw smoke and went to investigate. Old Walt's had some trouble."

"Comanche savages?"

"No, I'd say it was more in the nature of white savages," Carter replied icily. "I know whose handiwork it was, Farrell, and I swear some day I'll see you pay for it."

"You watch your words, Ross," Farrell barked. "There's those that say you're more to blame for all this trouble than old Harper. You could find yourself the same sort of trouble he did. You've got a pretty wife and growin' boys. That Indian boy howled real pretty when we set his feet in the fire. I'll bet that slop boy would sing just as pretty!"

Carter could hold back no longer. He reached up and tore Farrell from his horse. The two men wrestled in the dust a moment before Carter slammed a heavy right hand against Farrell's nose. Bone struck bone with a crunch, and Farrell cried out in pain. Carter shook the sting from his hand and glared angrily.

"You think Harper found trouble?" Farrell cried, holding his bleeding nose. "Well, he won't find anymore. That's for certain. I finally trapped that old Indian lover, caught him with one of the Ghost's Comanche boys. Shame we couldn't persuade 'em to tell us where the Ghost himself was, but we did the next best thing."

"You had no call to burn that boy's feet, to take his scalp."

"Don't talk to me about what I had call to do!" Farrell shouted. "You never saw what they did to my brother. Peeled him raw. Every night the rest of my life I'll hear his dyin' screams. You could sure save yourself a wagonload of trouble by tellin' me what's come of those other Comanches."

"To be honest about things, Farrell, I wish there were some Comanches around here. I'd lead 'em right to you, Farrell. I'd let 'em carve on you some. The world turns, you know. Could be it'll turn on you!"

"I'll be back one of these days and settle a score with you, Ross. I pay my debts."

"You bother me or mine, I'll pay *you*, Farrell. I'll plant a piece of lead in your head so neat you'll never know what killed you. This whole valley'll sing a song then."

Farrell laughed, then mounted his horse and sped off to the west. As he left, he hurled insults.

Carter paid them no attention. Instead he dipped his fists in cool well water and prepared to resume his work.

CHAPTER 15

FIVE days after old Walt Harper and Runs Long had breathed their last, smoke again blackened the horizon in Palo Pinto County. This time Carter Ross stayed at home. He grinned with some measure of satisfaction when Hadley Copeland brought word that Jasper Farrell's barn lay in ashes.

"It's Comanches for sure this time," Hadley explained. "Seems as if Gray Ghost is riding again."

Yes, Carter thought. One last time.

Farrell had been following a trail up Rock Creek far to the west when his barn was set afire. Furious, he rounded up a dozen men and chased the trail of the raiders. Again the Ghost eluded his pursuers. This time the phantom Comanche torched Farrell's house.

"Your luck seems to've turned bad, Farrell," Carter said when the riders came to Ross's Gap. "I wonder what the Indians will want to burn next."

"I'd curb my tongue, Ross!" Farrell shouted. "We all of us know who's in sympathy with Indians hereabouts."

"And we know why they've come back," Carter countered. "That's on account of one of our neighbors who enjoys torturing children."

They almost came to blows again, but Farrell backed his horse away. A bent nose and purple swelling below both eyes served as reminders of his previous tangle with Carter.

As it turned out, Farrell would have no other opportunity to clash with anyone. That night, while he was camped with five companions on the north bank of the Brazos, someone crept in and slit the old scout's throat.

136

"Maybe that Indian truly is a ghost," Ben Copeland told Carter afterward. "He walked right past three other men and killed old Jasper. They had a guard posted, too, and he saw nothin'. I don't see it's possible."

"Maybe Farrell did it to himself," Carter suggested. "Or the guard might have gotten tired of Farrell's big talk."

"No, it was those Comanches," Copeland declared. "Farrell was scalped, and his feet were, well, gone."

"Gone?" Carter asked in disbelief.

"Cut off. Lord, I saw it myself. I don't see how anybody could manage to cut off those feet and not rouse the others."

"I don't, either," Carter said, shaking at the specter of Jasper Farrell's footless body.

"There's just one thing to do now, Ross. We have to get ourselves organized and find these renegades. The cavalry's been notified. They promise to send a company when they can."

"I don't think there's a full company at Ft. Griffin," Carter pointed out. "The army thinks they've solved the Indian problem."

"They've got feet," Copeland grumbled. "I've talked to some of the others, and they're all for raisin' a company of militia. So to speak anyway. They offered me the captaincy, and I got to thinkin' how what we really need is a scout, a man experienced in trackin' who knows the country. You rode with Forrest. You know what's to be done."

"Seems to me it was while chasing false trails that Farrell lost his house and barn. He wound up with his throat slit. It'd be a better idea to wait 'em out, keep your people at home so they're ready in case trouble comes calling."

"Sit around and wait for 'em to burn your house, kill your kids?" Copeland cried. "I can't believe what you're sayin', Ross. Didn't you hear me just say they sneaked in and cut Jasper Farrell's feet off him while three men slept alongside? You really think those snakes can't slip past Hadley or maybe one of your youngsters?"

"I think if we give 'em half a chance, they'll move along and leave us in peace," Carter answered angrily. "They could as easily have killed those three men, but they didn't. That was a revenge raid. They struck Farrell because of that boy he killed at Walt's."

"You know a lot about this, Ross. It makes me uneasy. I've heard all these stories about you bein' raised Comanche, about your pa takin' a squaw for a wife and all. I know you've got a halfbreed brother because I met him during the war. None of it makes any sense to me. You're no more an Indian than I am. Shoot, that J. T.'s the whitest kid I've ever seen. I've spoken with your wife in church. Your boys go to school in town with Hadley, Moss, and the rest of the youngsters. And yet you won't ride with us!"

"No," Carter grumbled. "To you this is all new," Carter explained. "You're horrified to see a man with his feet cut off. I've seen men hit by artillery shells that there weren't enough pieces left of to fill a hat. This isn't some Saturday roundup you're talking about. If you take this trail, you'll find death and killing along the way. I've had my fill of it. I won't go to war again, not unless my family's at risk."

"They are."

"I don't see it that way, Copeland. And again I'll warn you not to stir up a hornet's nest. You can't tell who'll get stung."

Copeland shook his head and left. Carter read the bitterness in his neighbor's eyes.

"This will make it hard on the boys at school," Hope told him when he shared the news before dinner.

"And on you, too," Carter added. "Lord, if they would just bide their time. In a week the Kwahadis'd be gone."

"How can you be so sure?" she asked. "Johnny isn't the same anymore. He's changed. There was something new in his eyes when I spoke with him at Walt's burying."

"Hatred."

"More than that, Carter. Blind rage. The raiding is just beginning, I'm afraid."

Her words proved to be prophetic. Carter wondered what might have happened if Ben Copeland and others had kept to their houses and left the cavalry to chase the Indians north across the Red River. No one could ever be certain, but when Copeland searched the rocky ravines beyond the Brazos for a Comanche camp, Gray Ghost struck again.

First three farms north of the river were hit. A cow was run off, and several chickens were snatched. Later the Gillett hay barn was burned to the ground. Finally a dozen raiders struck a Diamond C line cabin, killing three drovers and stampeding stock over a twenty-mile square.

"This Ghost seems to know where we are and where we aren't!" a frustrated Ben Copeland complained. "He out-thinks us at every turn. And look at who's suffering. George Gillett's my militia lieutenant. He's punishin' us for bein' the leaders."

"Seems logical," Carter commented.

"Too much so for an Indian," Copeland declared.

And so spies were again posted atop Ross's Mountain. Carter kept close to the house, though, and the raids continued. It seemed half the county was burning. Neighbors pleaded for Carter to help. Others threatened.

"I told you before," Carter responded. "I'm through making war."

Each day thereafter, frustrated bands of riders passed through the gap in search of Gray Ghost's Comanches. Nary a glimpse was caught of the elusive quarry. Even when two squads of regular cavalry appeared, the Comanches continued to remain at large. Soon oldtimers spoke of Palo Pinto's "autumn of fire and blood."

Carter did his best to avoid the prowling neighbors and cavalry patrols. Between raising horses and tending children, he had enough to occupy his time.

"You can't ignore what's happening," Hope complained. "You may not like it, but we are a part of this valley, Carter. Can't you ride out and find Johnny, speak to him."

"It's too late for talk," Carter said sadly. "The war's begun. Besides, it's not just Johnny. There are others. If he talks for peace, they won't follow him."

"And what happens when they come here?"

"They won't."

"They have before. If they need horses or rifles, won't you give them to Johnny? They know that. Carter, you can't stand in the middle like this. One side or the other is bound to trample you underfoot."

He tried not to consider that possibility. As word came of larger raiding parties, of burned homes and dead settlers, Carter felt his heart grow cold. Each time a dead Indian was dragged toward town, Carter hoped it wasn't Johnny or Owl Eyes. The corpses were either turned over to the army or left with the sheriff until someone could be spared long enough to dig a grave. It was a simple matter for Brady or J. T. to steal a glance through the back window of the courthouse when they went into Palo Pinto for school.

"It wasn't them," Brady or J. T. would say when they returned.

Carter would nod sadly. There was relief in knowing Johnny remained alive, but it was hard to find pleasure knowing that another Kwahadi was dead.

Settlers were dying as well, and Hope often rode with the other women to bring food and offer comfort to the survivors. She sometimes returned, tired and bitter, and Carter would listen as she cried herself to sleep.

The boys, too, were shaken by the war sweeping across the county. Brady and J. T., being in town, were especially torn by news of death on both sides.

"How're we supposed to feel, Pa?" Brady asked him one night. "They've dragged six Comanches to the courthouse. Each time I worry it might be Uncle Johnny or Owl Eyes. Next time it might be."

"Everybody says terrible things about the Indians," J. T. added. "Well, I saw Runs Long myself. Nobody could do anything much worse than what those men did to him. And old Walt, too!"

"Shirley Loflin wasn't at school today," Brady said, walking a short distance away. "I liked her. She was quick with figures, and I used to joke with her a lot. She just had her eighth birthday. Hadley said the Comanches killed her last night. They scalped her, too. Poor little Shirley! It couldn't have been Uncle Johnny. She was such a little girl. He wouldn't do something like that."

"This is war, son," Carter said, frowning. "In a battle, people get riled, and sometimes they do things they regret later. If Johnny's with them, he would have little to say as to how a warrior acted. Even in Tennessee, I saw lots of cases when soldiers got excited and did some things I was ashamed to witness. Some were in my command. Men on the other side were as bad—or worse. It's the way war is, and it's why I'd keep you from seeing it yourselves."

"Pa, Hadley's pa says you're a coward," Brady said, leaning on Carter's shoulder. "It's hard to hear that kind of talk. I know it's not true, but everybody gets to saying it, and I just want to leave and never go back to that blamed school."

"Pa, we've read all the books. We could help here," J. T. pleaded.

"It's been your ma's dream that you boys go to school in town," Carter reminded them. "There are hard paths to walk in life, and this time it's you two must walk it."

"Yes, sir," Brady grumbled. J. T. nodded.

Two days later they returned from town early, though. Carter heard the horses and immediately set off to investigate.

"Pa, give us some time to wash up," Brady pleaded. "Ten minutes or so."

"What's happened?" Carter called, trotting to the barn. The boys had already dismounted and were trying to hide behind the wall. "Come on out, sons," Carter said, motioning them out into view.

Brady came first. His shirt had been torn from his chest. Cuts and bruises appeared on both arms and his chin. His chest was splattered with red paint.

J. T. was worse. Paint covered the younger boy's hair, face, chest, most of his arms, and back—even stained his trousers.

"They say we're Indians," J. T. said, fighting back the urge to sob. "They jumped us, the whole bunch. We held our own for a while, but when they all came at once, well . . ."

"Pa, we're not going back," Brady declared, kicking a rock down the road. "Look at this! It wasn't just the town boys, either. Hadley and Moss were in on it."

"They said the red paint was for us," J. T. said, trembling so that he had to lean against the wall to keep his balance. "They've got yellow paint for you."

"There's no need of you going back," Carter assured them. "This isn't the kind of learning your ma had in mind for you. Let's get you down to the creek and scrub this paint off. I believe it's time I rode over and spoke to Ben Copeland."

"You can't go alone, Pa!" Brady warned. "Wait for us."

"Seems to me you've fought your battle," Carter declared. "Now it's my turn."

Carter climbed atop Brady's horse and headed toward the creek. As he rode, he was glad not to have taken a rifle. Mad as he was, he would surely have shot Ben Copeland at the first opportunity. He hadn't yet reached the river, though, when he met Hadley riding slowly homeward.

"Good afternoon, Mr. Ross," the boy said nervously. "You headed for our place?"

"I thought it was about time I settled something with your pa," Carter barked. "Seems you and your friends had some fun today. He's got strong opinions, your pa. I guess it's time he had a chance to put aside his words and have it out with me."

"Mr. Ross, we've had a lot of trouble lately," Hadley tried to explain. "First, we finally got the stock all rounded up from that stampede, and the Comanches hit us again.

Burned the summer hay, and when they finished, they headed to the Loflin place and killed little Shirley. She was a particular favorite of Ma's. I'm sorry about what happened to Brady and J. T. It was my fault as much as anybody's. We were just a little crazy. That's all."

Carter didn't bother replying. Instead he continued riding. Hadley quietly fell in behind.

Once at the Copeland ranch, Carter slipped off his horse and marched toward the house. Ben Copeland appeared on the porch, smoking a pipe and chatting idly with a pair of cowboys. The three of them noticed Carter immediately. One of the cowboys drew a pistol. The other hurried down the steps and tried to cut Carter off. Carter flung the drover aside and continued.

"Stop right there!" the cowboy ordered, firing a warning shot in the air.

"You afraid to face me, Copeland?" Carter asked, his face flashing scarlet. "Well? You're mighty easy with your words when I'm not around. You send your kids to jump my boys in town. Come on, Copeland. You're so quick to call a man a coward. Come prove it!"

"Everybody knows you, Ross," Copeland answered. "For a while I was confused. I took your war service to account, but no longer. Jasper Farrell tried to warn us. Well, we all of us know where you stand now. Wouldn't surprise me any if you weren't ridin' with those red devils yourself!"

"You're a fool, Copeland," Carter said, suddenly charging up the steps. He knocked the gun from the second cowboy's hand, then flung the cowboy down the steps. Carter then pinned Ben Copeland against the wall and stared him face to face. "Raiding, you say?" Carter asked. "You know better. Hasn't been a day in weeks you haven't kept one of your hands watching my door."

"Those Indians always know what we're up to, where we're goin'."

"And since when did you ever tell me?" Carter argued.

"You fool! Look around you. There are hills and bluffs all over this country. This Ghost of yours just has to post a lookout here and there to see your each and every move. You ride in the open, along creeks, or up roads. It's no trouble to cut through the brush and double back on you. Don't ever go blaming me 'cause you're stupid!"

To add emphasis to his point, Carter slammed his right fist against Copeland's jaw, sending the rancher reeling.

"Hold it, Ross!" the first cowboy called out. The drover had recovered enough to fetch a shotgun which was now pointed at Carter's back.

"Put the gun down, Stoney!" Copeland ordered. "He's partly right. Thing is, Ross, I know I've got no experience fightin' Comanches. I came to you for help. We need you. By keepin' to your place, you've allowed these raids to continue. You're just as responsible for little Shirley and the others as I said."

"I told you before!" Carter shouted. "I've fought my war!"

"We need your help!"

"I've none to give!" Carter said as he mounted his horse and turned homeward. "Can't you understand? I've none to give!"

CHAPTER 16

CARTER met the boys down at the creek. Some of his rage had departed. In its place self-doubts began to surface. In a way Copeland was right. The Comanches relied on that blundering militia. Mackenzie or even Jasper Farrell would long ago have tracked the Kwahadi camp and put an end to the menace.

That's what will happen, too, Carter thought as he pulled his horse to a halt and climbed down onto a large boulder. The late September breeze had turned a bit cool, and the youngsters winced as they scrubbed off the paint in the chill waters of the creek.

"Not like midsummer, is it?" Carter asked.

"No, sir," J. T. said, shivering. "I can't tell whether this is red from the paint or pink from freezing."

"You have it out with Hadley's pa?" Brady asked.

"Guess you'd say so," Carter said, rubbing his bruised knuckles. "But I wouldn't say much is changed."

Brady frowned and went on scrubbing away. J. T. gazed sadly toward Antelope Mountain.

"If we just knew where to find Uncle Johnny, we could ask him to go west for a while," J. T. said. "People would forget what's happened."

"Some won't ever forget," Carter told them. "Those who've lost family will stay bitter, I fear. I confess my own heart's a bit sour on account of old Walt. And Nighthawk. And his sons."

"Is the reservation such a terrible place to go?" Brady asked. "There's land up there, too."

"Uncle Johnny said he'd die before he'd go there," J. T. muttered. "Called it a prison."

"It's hard to accept being told to stay in a particular place when you're used to roaming most of Texas," Carter explained. "But as things are now, he's not free, either. He hides from soldiers and ranchers. Come winter, life will be pitiful hard."

"Can't you ride out and tell him that?" J. T. asked.

"He knows," Carter answered. "I don't think he plans to be alive this winter."

"They'll kill him if they have half a chance," Brady observed. "Pa, you won't let 'em cut him up like they did those boys in the wagon, will you? Not like Buffalo Hump or Runs Long?"

"Not if I can help it," Carter promised.

Of course, what can I do to prevent it? he asked himself. It will happen on some lonely hillside north of the Brazos, most likely—a brief exchange of rifle fire, and Johnny will die.

An hour shy of dusk, the boys had managed to scrub most of the paint from their leathery hides. Flakes remained here and there, and in some places, the skin was rubbed raw, but Carter judged the worst of the indignity had been removed. He led the boys homeward. When they reached the house, Carter found a visitor waiting.

"I'm Bob Loflin," a frail-looking soft-spoken man said, shaking Carter's hand. "These are my boys, Douglas and Joshua."

"How are you, boys?" Carter asked, shaking the smallish hands of the children. Joshua was maybe four, and his brother looked to be six or seven.

"You suppose one of your sons might entertain these two while we talk?" Loflin asked.

Carter motioned to J. T., and the thirteen-year-old waved for the younger boys to follow him into the house.

"They're Shirley's brothers," Brady said, forcing a grin onto his face. "I liked her an awful lot."

"She liked you, too, Brady," Loflin replied. "Used to talk about how you could do figures in your head faster'n Mrs. Gill could write 'em on the slate."

"She was quick, too."

"Yes," Loflin said, sadly leading Carter toward the corral.

"I was sorry to hear of your bad luck," Carter whispered as they walked. "Lord, I thought we'd finished burying children when the war was over."

"I see in your eyes you mean that," Loflin observed. "I came out here to enlist your help. Three years ago my wife was killed when thieves raided the Trinity Crossing stage station. She was with child. Since then I've had three little ones to raise with nary a hand raised in help. Oh, Mrs. Copeland happens by, makes 'em a shirt or a bonnet. But I've done the washing and the cooking and worked my farm all the while. Now those boys are all I've got left. I won't have anything happen to 'em."

"I lost my ma when I was very small," Carter said. "My pa when I was fourteen. I know what it's like to fend for myself. My Hope and our children are my heart. I believe it'd kill me if harm came to 'em."

"I've heard many things about you, Mr. Ross. Some say you lead these Indians yourself. Others say you spy for 'em. But when I look at you, I just see a man who wants to be left alone. I understand that. I fought at Vicksburg. Two of my brothers died there.

"The thing is, I can't just leave you to yourself. My boys need your help. We need you to scout out these renegades, treat with 'em or kill 'em. Doesn't matter to me which. I just want 'em to leave me and mine be."

"You ask more than you think."

"No, I know full well it's a lot to ask a man to take up arms again."

"There's more to it."

"You mean your brother?"

Carter nodded, surprised that Loflin could possibly know of Johnny.

"I told you about my brothers," Loflin went on. "I didn't mention one wore gray and the other wore blue. Whenever I fired my musket, I dreaded the thought that I might hit Henry. And when I discovered he died at Vicksburg, I was haunted for a year by nightmares. He chose his side, though, and I chose mine."

"A man with a Comanche mother does no choosing," Carter declared. "Others make the choice for him. Me, I have no heart for any of this."

"You have to come with us. We need you, and in a way you need us, too. Mustangers don't have long before the open range is all fences. Wild horses will disappear like buffalo. You'll run cattle, refine your string of horses, and sell to neighbors. Like I say, you'll need us. And right now, we need you."

"I can't," Carter pleaded.

"You can, and you will because you have to. Lives depend on it. And if you lead us, you might just be able to bring peace instead of war. Speak with these Comanches, offer 'em cattle and horses to leave. I'll make the offer good myself."

"They're not fighting because of livestock."

"They won't drive us all off our land, Ross. You know that. And the cavalry's bound to kill 'em eventually. Offer 'em stock and peace—and life. They can't wish to hurry death."

No? Carter asked himself. There were many kinds of death. One was to lose the old ways. But how could a simple farmer like Loflin comprehend such a thing? A farmer's whole life relied on change, growth, progress.

"Don't delay deciding," Loflin urged. "This county's got too few children left as is. Don't let any more die."

Carter summoned the little Loflin boys, and they joined their father on his wagon. As they headed homeward, Carter recounted his conversation to Hope.

"I've been thinking the same thing myself," she said. "Go

with them, Carter. Try to persuade Johnny to come in. It's time these raids were ended. Jasper Farrell's dead. Let's put a stop to this senseless killing."

I wish I could, Carter thought.

Early the following morning he saddled his horse and rode out through the gap, past reminders of a childhood too early left behind. He climbed the rugged slope of Antelope Mountain and gazed sadly at the ashes of Walt Harper's cabin. There had been some happy times there, winters of laughter and summers of growing. He remembered digging the well, building the barn, hunting deer in the thickets, and enduring blizzards.

Old Walt's gone, Carter told himself. It seemed impossible. The old-timer's laughter echoed on the wind, and his words flowed through Carter's memory. Carter wandered for a time. When he looked up, he found himself slowly climbing the cliff to where Nighthawk's scaffold stood.

"What could have brought us to this, old friend?" Carter whispered. "Was it so long ago that you taught me to track? There's the bow I borrowed. Who could have thought you'd rest here with your sons when the three of you should have been riding the Llano, chasing buffalo?"

Now there were only buffalo ghosts. Ghosts! Weren't all the Comanches ghosts now, shadows of what used to be, phantoms to be shared in winter tales spun by grandfathers?

When Carter returned to the house, he found Reverend Hollings there. The preacher thanked Hope for a cup of coffee, then took Carter's arm and led him aside.

"I came to say how sorry I was to hear of your decision to keep the boys from school," Hollings said. "Brady was such a help with the younger children. Mrs. Gill lacks the aptitude for mathematics, I fear, though she is a wonder with grammar and history."

"That was their choice," Carter explained. "They weren't exactly made to feel welcome."

"Yes, children can be so cruel."

"They learn from listening to their elders," Carter said, frowning. "There's altogether too much hatred in this country."

"Yes, there is. It's one of the reasons I came here. I wished to light the way with the word of God. Still, when little children like Shirley Loflin are killed, it's bitter hard to love thy neighbor and forgive those wrongs they do us."

"You didn't ride all the way out here to preach love to me, did you?"

"Perhaps not. I did wish to urge forgiveness. You trouble me, Carter Ross. I know something about you. You never shirked your duties in the late unpleasantness, even though many along the frontier placed their own needs above those of their country. I understand you were a colonel of cavalry under General Forrest."

"Not quite all it sounds, Reverend. I was a lieutenant until Selma. Then, with most of the officers in the regiment whittled away, they promoted me colonel."

"Even so, you know how to lead men. You have a head for tactics, and no one knows this country better. You were born here."

"No, in the Carolinas. I came west with my pa. He was a major in the Second U.S. Cavalry."

"Well, you've spent most of your life here then," the preacher said.

"True enough."

"With Jasper Farrell gone, there's no one here who knows the ways of the Comanches or their likely hiding places. Except perhaps you. It seems to me that you should accept a position of leadership and rid our land of this scourge which had descended upon us."

"I've got a lot of work, even with the boys back home."

"They've made great steps toward becoming a part of our community. As has Hope. Maybe it's time you do the same. Consider it carefully. There will be a meeting tomorrow at dawn over at Jasper Farrell's old place. You'll come?"

"I'll think about it."

"I ask no more. Good day, and God bless you."

Carter nodded gravely, then watched the minister return to Hope. They spoke a few minutes. Then the reverend climbed atop his buggy and headed back toward town.

"He wants me to join the others," Carter told her.

"I know," she said, wrapping an arm around his weary shoulders. "He's right, Carter. We can't continue to stand alone."

"You realize Johnny's likely with those Indians?"

"Yes, but we have to live here, Carter. These people are our neighbors, our friends."

"When have they ever been our friends? We're barely tolerated in town, and the children aren't welcome in school. Have you forgotten the sewing circle? Did you see the look in Brady's eyes when those friends and neighbors of yours poured paint over him?"

"Maybe all that will change," she said, more hopefully than with any great degree of confidence. "We have to start someplace."

"You ask a lot."

"I know," she said, holding him tightly. "That's because I love you so much."

He frowned and held her. Tears trickled down her cheeks and dribbled across his chin. He shook with emotion.

Early the next morning he saddled his horse and fought back a wave of bitterness. He was not a little angry.

"Please, Carter," Hope had begged an hour before. "Go with them. Put an end to this horror."

He could never refuse her. And now he felt as if his heart was being rent into pieces. It was a sort of death he was riding to, the ending of all that was once so bright and cherished. And if Johnny fell . . .

"Pa?" Brady called.

"Yes, son," Carter answered.

"Ma says you're going after the Comanches."

"I hope to talk 'em into stopping their raids."

"They won't," J. T. declared, joining them. "Owl Eyes told me. They'll ride till they're all killed."

"That was a while back. Winter's coming. Minds can change."

J. T. was clearly unconvinced. Carter himself had grave doubts.

"You won't be gone long, not like during the war, will you?" Brady asked.

"It won't take long," Carter assured them.

"Pa, I don't understand," J. T. complained. "You said you could never do it. Uncle Johnny's out there."

"Yes," Carter admitted. "But sometimes a man does a thing against his feelings, son. Johnny raids because he sees himself a Kwahadi, and he doesn't see another road he can ride. Me, I go because like it or not, I'm a rancher with a family to protect."

"The Indians would never harm us," J. T. argued.

"They have already," Carter told them. "You think I can forget that red paint, the hateful looks people give your mother? It's time that came to an end."

"Even if Uncle Johnny and Owl Eyes have to die?" Brady asked.

"They will anyway," Carter grumbled. "That's the hardest part of all, boys. They'll die no matter what I do. All I can hope for is to salve some of the bitterness, prevent some of the suffering."

"And maybe you can talk 'em into making peace," J. T. suggested.

"Maybe," Carter said, managing a faint smile.

"I hope so," Brady added.

"Me, too," Carter said as he climbed into the saddle. But even as he waved farewell to the boys, he knew it was a forlorn hope at best.

CHAPTER 17

WHEN Carter arrived at the charred shell of the Farrell house, he discovered two dozen or so riflemen assembled there. Few said a word as he walked past them.

"Glad you decided to join us," Bob Loflin whispered.

"Morning, Mr. Ross," Hadley Copeland said.

Others were less kind.

"He doesn't belong here," one said.

"Changin' sides, Ross?" another asked.

Carter paid them little attention. He was more concerned with Reverend Hollings's words.

"Friends, we've come together today to meet the common foe," the reverend began. "Many among us have suffered grievous losses as a result of repeated savage raids. Some have lost livestock. Others have seen their homes burned. A few have buried loved ones. Look around you at the ashes of a man's dream. Here lived Jasper Farrell, a fine man who many of you knew well. Do I need remind you of the terrible fate he suffered at the hands of these murderers? No, I think not. As we set out today, let us cast aside our doubts and our fears. Let God's justice lead you to success. Find the heathen enemy and smite him fiercely."

"Amen!" the assembled ranchers shouted.

Carter noticed, though, that the loudest shouters were those who didn't plan to ride. The reverend hadn't meant the "we" to be taken too seriously. He, of course, would remain in town.

Once Reverend Hollings completed his speech, Ben Copeland called the group to attention.

"Let's get organized, boys," he urged. "Most of you know how this militia of ours works."

Copeland began issuing orders and giving instructions. Carter closed his ears to it all. Instead he watched the sun rise out of the hills to the east. It burned amber, then blazed a scarlet trail into a layer of low clouds. For a moment the whole sky turned red.

Blood red, Carter thought. Was there ever a more appropriate beginning to a day? It was apt to end every bit as bloody.

"Ross, can't you listen even a little bit?" Copeland growled.

"Like as not he's hearing' every word," Thad Mullins, who ran the town bakery, said. "He'll want to share our plans with his Comanche brothers."

"Yeah," some of the others echoed angrily.

"You ride out with thirty men, I won't have to," Carter told them. "Dust alone would warn a buzzard twenty miles away. Comanches can smell you that far. Don't you know they've got eyes on every one of these hills? They know where you are, and they'll follow your movements easily enough."

"You'd be the one to know," Mullins remarked.

"Look, I was asked here," Carter explained. "I'd as soon ride with you as walk through a den of rattlers. I come out of duty, not some deep taste for shedding blood. I've seen more killing and dying than any one man should witness in a dozen lifetimes!"

"As have many of us," Bob Loflin added sadly. "So far as Ross is concerned, I'd say he's got a point. Listen to him. He knows Comanches, and he's fought battles."

The others grumbled, but Copeland waved Carter over.

"So how would you do it?" Copeland asked.

"To begin with, I'd send these youngsters home," Carter told them. "Moss there is what, twelve? Pete Haskell's even younger. They'll wear out 'fore we finish, and somebody'll have to take 'em back."

"I've gone with Pa before," Moss Copeland argued.

"You haven't found any Comanches before," Carter retorted. "Besides, there's always the odd chance we could miss 'em. Then you'd be needed at home."

Moss nodded grimly, then led his horse off toward the river.

"What else?" Copeland asked.

"Split into threes and fours to scout the country. Meet around noon. Do the same thing in the afternoon if we don't cross a trail. The main thing is to avoid open country. Stay clear of the roads. You're too easy to spot that way. Ride cross-country, and keep to the rocks and trees."

"If we find somebody, should we fire three shots like before?" Hadley asked.

"You do," Carter explained, "and the Comanches may have you instead. No, if you find a trail, follow it from cover. Send somebody to the meeting spot so the rest can follow later. The secret's to find the camp. Once we surround it, we can warn 'em to surrender or face attack."

"I'd rather hit 'em then and there," Mullins complained.

"And how many men are you willing to lose? Comanches aren't much for fightin' with their women and children at hand. Most of these Kwahadis turned themselves in at the reservation last winter. They're not the ones to choose death, I'd wager."

"Gray Ghost will never surrender," Copeland declared. "We find him, I'm for shootin' first and then talkin' surrender."

"You hit their camp by surprise, the whole bunch will fight you," Carter warned. "You never dealt with a whole band. These raids are carried on by small groups, five or six for the most part. You take on a whole camp, you're sure to keep the coffinmakers busy."

Carter stared hard at the faces around them. Copeland grumbled, but in the end he agreed. Then Carter helped divide the men into five bands of five each. The hills to the northwest were judged the most likely spot for Gray Ghost's camp, so the patrols spread out in that direction.

Carter rode with Loflin, the McDowell brothers—Barney and Cooper—plus Thad Mullins, who insisted on keeping an eye on Carter.

"Wouldn't want him slippin' away to warn his friends," Mullins said, laughing.

Carter restrained the urge to flatten the loud-mouthed baker and instead led his companions westward toward the river. They would have five hours to search seven square miles of rugged country. At noon everyone was to meet at the mouth of Rock Creek out west on the Brazos.

It was slow going. Carter tried to fan his little command out, but Loflin was uncertain in the saddle and hung close at hand. The McDowells had been up the trail to Kansas twice, and they moved twenty yards to either side of Carter. Mullins, for all his talk, was a pure tenderfoot at riding broken country. After trailing along behind Coop McDowell the first quarter mile, Mullins, too, pulled alongside Carter.

"Wouldn't want to lose sight of you," the baker declared. "I've heard how Comanches mark trees and send signals with mirrors."

"I don't have a mirror, and though I've heard of marking a trail by notching trees, I don't see how that would help a Comanche much."

"I'll watch him," Loflin added. "You go back to the Mc-Dowells."

Mullins made no effort to leave, though, and Carter laughed to himself. They'd have been better off keeping Moss Copeland and sending Mullins back to town.

Carter kept his patrol scouting the rocky hills above the river. Twice he detected campfires, but they were cold and most likely deserted since summer. He found no fresh trails. Except for a pair of jackrabbits and a covey of quail, they found no sign of life.

"If you ask me, he's leadin' us away from his friends,"

Mullins complained. "He knows there are no Comanches out this way."

"Look, Mullins," Carter answered, "you're welcome to take off on your own and find any Comanche you can. Hanging back of Loflin, you're clearly doing us no good. If you know so much, why don't you set off by yourself and scare the whole batch of raiders back to the reservation?"

The McDowells laughed, and even Loflin managed a grin.

"I follow orders," Mullins explained. "Cap'n Copeland assigned me to ride with this group."

"You assigned yourself," Carter reminded the baker. "Why don't you just be quiet and watch for sign?"

Mullins kept quiet the remainder of the morning. It made little difference so far as the search was concerned, but the quiet allowed Carter to listen to the distant songs of mourning doves and the livelier tune of a cardinal.

"Spot anything?" Ben Copeland asked when Carter led his band to the midday rendezvous.

"Saw lots," Carter answered, "but not a bit of it hinted Comanches were around."

"He never intended to find anything," Mullins grumbled.

"We'd done better if you and Loflin hadn't hung to Ross's coattails," Cooper McDowell remarked. "You're next to useless, Mullins. Why don't you go back to town?"

"No," Copeland objected. "We need every man we have."

"Man?" Carter asked. "He's a poor excuse for one at best, and I'd hate to trust my life on him doing as he's told."

"Mullins, you'll ride with me this afternoon," Copeland ordered. "Hadley, you take his place with Ross here."

"Pa?" the young man asked. "I thought we'd stick together."

"You'll come to no harm with us, Hadley," Loflin assured the fifteen-year-old. "In truth, you'd be quite a help."

Hadley frowned, but he argued no further.

That afternoon the search spread out on both banks of Rock Creek. Carter led his party west, beyond the creek into a tangle of ravines and sandstone boulders. Most of the time the country was near impassible. Carter always found a route, though, and the others followed.

"I've been here before," Carter told them. "There are several good spots up ahead for making a camp. There's plenty of wood, fish in the river, and the rocks shield it from view."

The others tensed, and Carter heard their breathing quicken. But each spot was deserted.

He knows me too well, Carter thought. He'll avoid the river and the open country around the creeks. And so Carter turned back northward, and they scouted the deserted grassland west of Rock Creek. Twice the McDowell brothers detected trails cut across the open ground, but both were long cold.

Toward dusk Carter reluctantly turned back to Rock Creek. It had been a long, fruitless search with nothing to show for all their effort. The other bands had been no more successful, and many of the men threw their hands up in disgust and headed for warm beds and wives' cooking.

"What now?" Copeland asked.

"To stage these raids, their camp couldn't be much more than fifteen or twenty miles away," Carter declared, chewing a cold biscuit. "I can't imagine 'em being south of the Brazos. We've pretty well covered west. Tomorrow we ride north. The day after, we go east."

"We will find 'em, won't we?" Copeland asked.

"Unless you really are chasing a ghost," Carter said grimly. "Yes, we'll find 'em."

"And then we'll kill 'em," Mullins cried.

"First we treat with 'em," Carter argued. "We fight only if we have to."

"Oh, sure," Mullins agreed, laughing. "You talk all you want. Then I shoot."

Carter turned to Copeland, but the militia captain only shook his head.

"Mullins, you fire on 'em before I finish, I'll kill you myself," Carter promised.

"Wouldn't be the first time you've helped Indians kill a white man, I'll bet," Mullins said, grinning at the others.

Carter didn't bother replying. Instead he stamped over to the baker and drove a well-directed right hand into his forehead. Mullins toppled to the ground.

"You all saw that!" Mullins shouted, scrambling away as Carter prepared to swing again. "I told you. He's an Indian-lover."

"And what are you?" Barney McDowell asked. "A liar and a bushwhacker by the look of you. You'd best do as Ross says. Elsewise, we'll have to dig an extra grave."

Laughter greeted that remark, and Mullins glared at Carter.

It's men like him that start most of the trouble a man faces in his lifetime, Carter thought. Most times they themselves never suffer so much as a scratch. Not so others.

After dinner, the remaining men spread out their blankets above the creek and prepared to catch some badly needed sleep. A guard was mounted in shifts, and those not keeping the first watch climbed into their blankets and shut their eyes.

The night proved as uneventful as the day, and except for keeping his two-hour watch, Carter enjoyed a restful sleep. For a change his dreams were not troubled. Exhaustion had a way of bringing on a sound sleep. And when they mounted up in the morning, Carter walked with a quicker step and a lighter heart.

"Think we'll find something today, Mr. Ross?" Hadley asked.

"I'd guess so," Carter told the young man. "If I was looking to keep from view, I'd head for the gorge up north where Rock Creek deepens. Lots of little hollows out that way."

"You figure they'll fight?"

"I hope not," Carter muttered. "But I figure some will.

Come time for the shooting, Hadley, you stay behind me or your pa. You could get yourself killed real quick."

"I've been shot at before, remember?"

"Last time you had a house to shield you, and the shots were coming from boys younger'n you. This time you'll find it different. Do as I say, son. I've buried boys your age of late, and it's a bitter hard thing to do."

"I wouldn't enjoy it much myself," Hadley replied, grinning.

Carter laughed, then headed out into the tangled ravines. He'd gone less than a hundred yards when he spotted a clear trail.

"Over here!" Hadley cried, and Ben Copeland quickly collected the other parties and turned them toward where Hadley was waving his hat.

"Might be best next time to fire a cannon so even the Comanches on the reservation can hear you," Carter scolded.

"I figured everybody should come," Hadley explained. "The tracks are fresh, aren't they? I'd guess twenty riders. Maybe more. It's them."

Ben Copeland arrived and quickly confirmed his son's observations.

"What're we waitin' for?" Mullins called. "Let's go!"

"Don't you think you ought to know who you're chasing?" Carter objected.

"We know," Copeland told him. "Comanches. Can't be anyone else. If we hurry, we can catch 'em before the men head out for the day."

Carter frowned. Comanches weren't bankers to set off to work after breakfast. But as Copeland formed the others and started up the trail at a gallop, Carter decided to keep his views to himself. Copeland would discover the truth soon enough.

"I don't guess you'll have your chance to talk with the

Indians after all," Bob Loflin said. "Come on. We're falling behind."

"No hurry. Let's have ourselves a look farther north."

"Come on," Loflin said, slapping his horse into a gallop and leading the way up the trail.

Thad Mullins led the others. A more experienced scout would have noticed the well-ordered spacing of the tracks, the fact that two parallel lines of horses had cut the trail in the dusty ground.

Carter grinned as he watched the baker charging across a hill, eager to descend on the Comanche camp he envisioned just beyond.

"What are you laughing at?" Loflin asked impatiently.

"Oh, just that even a fool ought to know Comanches don't ride in a column of twos," Carter explained.

Loflin examined the trail and shook his head in disbelief.

"Thad! Ben! Hold up!" Loflin shouted.

It was too late. A dozen ranchers charged down the far hill into the camp of a contingent of cavalry out of Ft. Griffin. Two sentries fired warning shots, and Thad Mullins's horse bolted in response to the gunfire. Mullins himself was thrown into a particularly nasty stand of pencil cactus. The baker howled in pain, and his companions hooted their displeasure at Mullins's premature charge.

"What in the devil do you men think you're doing?" a young lieutenant asked angrily. "Well?"

"We've been searching for Comanches," Copeland explained.

"We look like Indians?" the lieutenant asked. "I'd say not. Why don't you fools go home and leave the Indians to us. You've likely scared any nearby all the way to Kansas by now. Fools!"

The soldiers shouted insults, and Copeland's face grew scarlet.

"You knew all the time, didn't you?" Copeland asked when Carter appeared.

"I did," Carter answered. "If you'd done as promised and let me ride ahead, I would've saved you this embarrassment."

"We will next time," Copeland promised.

"That's good, because while you were charging down this hill, I picked up a trail leading up the creek. Two, maybe three riders, but I'd say they were returning to camp, probably from scouting our company last night."

"Comanches?" Copeland asked. Carter nodded. "Then lead the way," Copeland urged.

"Follow me," Carter replied.

CHAPTER 18

THE Comanche trail twisted and turned through rocky washes and rugged hillsides. By nightfall Carter still had not located a camp. His exhausted companions could barely stay in the saddle, and Copeland announced the need to make camp.

"If we stop now, we could lose 'em altogether," Carter warned.

"There's no hope of continuing," Loflin declared. "Look at us. Even if we found an Indian camp, we'd be too weary to attack."

Carter sighed. He hadn't planned to attack. In truth, he was tempted to continue alone, but that would breed suspicion. If the Comanches broke camp and scattered, Carter had no doubt he would be saddled with the blame.

So instead, Carter Ross spread his blankets beneath a willow and chewed the last of the dried beef and biscuits Hope had put in his provision bag. Tomorrow, whether Indians were sighted or not, they'd have to return home. Nearly all the provisions were exhausted, and the men were worn out.

It was a quiet, clear night. A gentle breeze blew down from the north, softly stirring the tall, yellowing buffalo grass. The creek played host to a chorus of bullfrogs, and an occasional splash betrayed their location. The stars overhead sparkled against an ebony sky.

Carter tried to catch some rest, but instead a hundred memories flooded his mind. It was on a night like this one that Brady had been born. While an old Kwahadi woman tended Hope, Carter and Johnny had walked along Ioni

163

Creek. It had been hard to tell who was more nervous. And when at last a single whine had pierced the awful silence, they'd celebrated by throwing each other in the creek.

"You have a son," Hope had announced proudly when the soggy brothers finally appeared at her side.

"Soon we must take him to hunt the buffalo," Johnny had said excitedly. "He'll grow tall and strong with the summer sun, and all that's best will come to him."

That had been before war had torn Carter away, before Mackenzie shot the ponies and despair fell upon the Kwahadis.

Johnny had been there when John Tyler was born, too. J. T. had arrived on a storm-struck afternoon. Carter had rocked Brady to sleep as Hope suffered through a difficult time.

"To be born of the summer storm's a sure sign of great power," Johnny declared. "His heart'll be that of the panther. We'll take those boys to hunt the deer and the buffalo. Ah, we'll have some remembered times."

They had, too, Carter told himself. And now it was Carter's fate to lead Johnny's enemies to him.

Carter glanced around at the others. Most were huddled in their blankets. Mullins sat on a boulder beside the creek, keeping watch on the far bank. Of course, Comanches would come from the rocks and trees. It would be a simple matter to slip in and take the drowsy Mullins from behind.

Carter stared past Mullins at the distant hills. Rock Creek wound through the rocks and trees for miles, providing sheltered havens aplenty. Johnny and the Comanches would be up there. Carter wondered if their camp was as quiet, as at peace. Or did little Owl Eyes watch the distant rocks with dread anticipation of the riders who would come? Was Johnny also recalling those earlier, happier days?

The time for remembering was past, though. Carter knew that. He closed his eyes and fought to find some peace. It didn't come. Instead he was gripped with a terrible chill, and he pulled the blankets tight against his chest.

It proved to be another restless night. Each snap of a twig or hoot of an owl roused him to his feet. He would then prowl the camp a bit, check the guard, and finally return to his blankets. When the sun first flooded the eastern horizon with its crimson glow, Carter rose red-eyed and exhausted.

"How do we go about it?" Copeland asked as Carter saddled his horse.

"Stay together today," Carter advised. "Let me ride a bit ahead and locate the camp. Then I'll come back and get the rest of you."

"Take Hadley," Copeland suggested. "That way you can watch the camp, and he can fetch the rest of us."

"I still mean to treat with 'em, you know," Carter said. "I'm not forgetting what happened at the cavalry camp. You ride past me, I'll spread the alarm myself."

"That wouldn't be too healthy."

"For who?" Carter asked, his eyes blazing. "You've tangled with me once, remember? I'm not a man to take lightly."

"There are a full dozen of us, Ross," Copeland reminded Carter. "You can't mean to stand against us all."

"I've faced longer odds. With two pistols and a Winchester I can fill a lot of you with holes. Think on that, Copeland. Don't be a fool. We've got a common interest in resolving this business. You needn't end up with a massacre, you know."

"You go ahead and talk," Copeland agreed. "Only wait till we close in around 'em."

"Wouldn't be much point to demanding a surrender if you boys were back in Palo Pinto."

So Carter and young Hadley Copeland headed out in front of the others. At first Carter kept but a quarter mile lead. But the others stirred dust and chatted loudly. Carter moved on until he could no longer see or hear the others.

Hadley's face betrayed concern, but the young man said nothing. Carter might have explained himself to Brady or

J. T., but no words would ever completely sweep away Hadley's suspicions. It was better to concentrate on the trail and locate the camp.

Carter found his first traces of a larger band about a half mile shy of Yucca Springs. Instead of tracking a handful of horses, the soft sand bore dozens of impressions. Near the creek, fresh stumps attested to the cutting of oaks and willows. A hundred yards farther along, splashes in the creek alerted Carter to bathers.

"There," Hadley whispered, pointing to a pair of small boys racing naked through the shallows of Rock Creek. Their brown skins, squat bodies, and raven-black hair betrayed them as Indian.

Carter nodded, then climbed down from his horse. As he prepared to scout the approaches to the springs, he motioned Hadley back down the trail.

"Time to bring the rest along," Carter whispered. "Hadley, have 'em leave their horses here and come the rest of the way on foot. I'll meet you at the top of this next hill."

Hadley nodded, then turned his horse and returned down the trail. Carter concealed his horse in the trees, tying the reins to a sturdy juniper branch. He then moved on to scout the camp.

Carter Ross was well acquainted with Yucca Springs. He and Johnny had camped there many an autumn while hunting deer in the adjacent thickets. It was a good place, well sheltered from the wind and close to both wood and water. Carter knew without looking that Johnny would have the lodges arranged in a circle with the opening facing the creek. Carter crept through the trees to the top of the hill more to count heads than to determine the layout of the camp.

There were eight lodges—not the traditional cones formed by spreading stitched buffalo hides or deerskins over a framework of poles. These lodges were makeshift shelters of thatched limbs covered by bark, buffalo grass, yucca mats, or leaves.

He counted some three dozen horses grazing between the camp and the creek. There would be a like number of Indians, perhaps a third of them men. The camp held a number of women and small children. Aside from the boys chasing each other at the creek, four of the eldest tended the ponies. Two women washed clothing downstream, and several others stirred pots or minded children. The few men Carter saw were making arrows on the far side of the camp.

Johnny wasn't there. Carter's first reaction was relief that his brother would escape the coming confrontation. On the other hand, so long as Johnny remained at large, nothing at all was settled. More than anything, Carter wanted the violence to come to an end. He wanted to return to Hope and the children, wished to resume his life.

He met Hadley and the others halfway down the hill. Mullins and some of the others chatted nervously, and Carter hushed them.

"Watch closely," Carter whispered, taking a twig and sketching the camp in the sand. "Three men should position themselves on each quarter of the camp. The rest should drive off the horses and cut off retreat toward the creek."

"And what'll you do?" Mullins asked.

"Wait for you to take your places," Carter explained. "Then I'll tell 'em how things stand and pray to high heaven they'll give up."

"They won't," Coop McDowell declared. "We'll have to take that camp."

"Then keep in mind there are mostly women and little kids down there," Carter said sourly. "They're not the enemy."

"They will be," Mullins argued.

"Nobody spared my little girl," Bob Loflin added.

"It's a powerful bitterness that would bring a man to kill a child," Carter said, more to Loflin than to the others. "You'll see faces in your dreams so long as you live. Killing a man's bad enough."

Loflin's eyes showed only a burning rage, though, and Carter saw the words were wasted. He waved the others along, and they made their way into the brush, snapping limbs and scattering leaves. Carter expected the camp to react, but the Comanches were preoccupied with their labors or their games and failed to detect the encircling riflemen. Finally all was ready, and Carter stepped out into the open and hailed them.

"You people down there!" he called. "You're surrounded. Give it up and we'll see you safely to the reservation. The cavalry's only a mile away. Fight, and you'll all of you die. Even the little ones."

The others screamed out their agreement. Women and children scrambled to safety, and the men stared around in confusion. Carter repeated his words in the Kwahadi dialect, but those words brought no response, either. Finally there was a stirring in the center lodge, and an all-too-familiar figure emerged into the daylight. Limping, his left arm in a sling, Johnny Ross stepped toward his brother.

"It's their choice to stay here, to die in these hills where the Kwahadi have always lived!" Johnny shouted.

"Death is a poor choice!" Carter shouted.

Someone on the hillside fired then, and within minutes the camp was torn apart by bullets. Men, women, and children raced like rabbits in search of escape. The horses bolted across the creek. Thad Mullins led two others in a wild charge. Two Kwahadis rose calmly and shot the baker dead. His two companions avoided a second volley.

Most of the Indians in the camp found cover and returned the gunfire coming from the surrounding hillsides. The Comanches down at the creek were less fortunate. The two boys caught in midstream howled defiantly and charged, naked and defenseless, at the men chasing the ponies away. Both were torn apart by shotgun blasts. The women washing clothes were luckier. Barney McDowell took them captive.

"Give it up!" Carter pleaded.

The words were swallowed by the discharge of pistols and rifles. Powder smoke swirled around the lodges, and Johnny disappeared from view.

Carter felt sick, but he swallowed his disgust and slowly circled to his left. Years before, a rock slide had left a natural wall of boulders leading to the spring, and Carter used the rocks for cover. Suddenly he came face to face with a young Kwahadi perhaps as old as Owl Eyes. The boy's piercing brown eyes were full of fear as he notched an arrow in his bow.

"It's not your time to die, son," Carter spoke softly in the tongue of the Kwahadi, in words taught him so long ago in Nighthawk's camp. "Set aside your bow. Live to see tomorrow."

The boy glanced behind him at a pair of small girls cowering beside an old woman. Then the boy softly chanted and raised his bow.

Carter darted to his left as an arrow tore past his ear and splintered against a boulder.

"No!" Carter pleaded as the boy grimly notched a second arrow.

Slowly, reluctantly, Carter aimed his pistol and fired at the boy's shoulder. The bullet struck the youngster's chest instead and knocked him instantly to the ground. The chanting ceased. The boy was dead.

"Oh, Lord," Carter mumbled as he raced ahead. A second young Kwahadi raced up the hill, and Carter knocked the boy aside.

"Good work!" Copeland called out as he wove his way through the trees and joined Carter at the edge of the camp. "I'll finish these."

"No, you won't!" Carter screamed with blazing eyes. "Enough have died. Look at 'em! They're half-starved and scared to death. There's no more fight in 'em!"

Loflin arrived then, and Carter turned the unconscious boy, the old woman, and the two little girls over to his care.

"You trust me to guard them?" Loflin asked.

"I saw how you held those boys of yours," Carter explained. "You're no murderer of little girls and old women."

"And him?" Loflin asked, pointing to the stunned boy.

"Best bind his arms. He's as like as not to claw you. Was no fear in his eyes."

Loflin took his bandana and started on the boy's hands. Carter turned and crept along into the camp.

By now three of the lodges blazed brightly—whether set afire by Indian or rancher, it was hard to tell. The skirmish had moved along toward the creek, though, and Carter wove his way past blazing thatch and abandoned pots to a boulder-strewn area above the creek. On the far side the McDowell brothers were hotly engaged with several Kwahadi riflemen. On the opposite side the surviving women and children huddled in terror. Guarding them was a single, slender boy approaching his fourteenth winter. Carter recognized Owl Eyes even though the boy had painted his face black as death.

"It's over," Carter called, approaching the boy with arms extended to his sides. "Finished."

Owl Eyes glanced around to see if Carter had company. The other ranchers were busy looting the camp, collecting ponies, and fighting the warriors on the other side of the boulders.

"You chose your path," Owl Eyes said grimly. "As we have."

"You're the last of your father's blood," Carter said, his eyes growing moist. "Nighthawk took me in as a boy, nursed my wounded heart, and gave me strength. I sang to his dead spirit, remember? I won't kill his son."

"Then go," Owl Eyes shouted. "Others will."

"I know," Carter admitted, hanging his head. "And what of all these others? Is it their day to die as well?"

"They choose to be here," the boy explained.

"To die?" Carter cried. "I understand what it is to seek a brave death, but this is no better than walking bare-shoul-

dered into the snows of winter. A warrior fights for his life.
He doesn't cast it aside like an old moccasin."

Owl Eyes grew solemn. The women drew their children
close as Carter approached. His eyes held no hatred, though,
and they gazed up with surprise as he stepped past them
and joined Owl Eyes.

"Something of the old ways should survive," Carter declared. "Something. It's inside you, here," Carter added,
touching the boy's sweat-streaked chest. "Come with me. Stay
in my house. Grow tall in the sunlight."

"I am Kwahadi," the boy spoke, stepping back and raising
his rifle. "I don't know how to be a white man."

"I'll teach you," Carter promised. "I'll teach you as your
father taught me to hunt the buffalo and ride the swiftest
ponies."

Owl Eyes trembled, and a tear etched a thin line through
the oily black paint on his face.

"I know it's a lot to ask," Carter said. "It will be hard. But
life is hard."

"Yes," Owl Eyes said, his hands shaking badly.

Carter took the rifle and drew the boy to his side. The
others looked on anxiously, their eyes full of confusion. Even
now, bullets whined off rocks 200 yards away as the last
resisting warriors fought off a determined enemy.

"It's all right," Carter spoke to the women and little ones.
"He is my uncle's son and has wintered in my lodge."

The confusion remained, but Carter said nothing more.
He ushered Owl Eyes and the others along the creek. While
the Indians eased their thirst and bathed assorted scrapes
and bruises, Owl Eyes washed away the paint from his face
and arms. The distant gunfire echoed down the valley, its
ghostly song haunting them all until at last the final shots
were fired.

"It's over," Carter said sadly.

"It was a remembered fight," Owl Eyes declared. "He also
was my father."

"And my brother," Carter replied, rubbing his eyes.

Owl Eyes chanted softly, but Carter didn't join the boy this time. His sorrow would wait for another, more private moment.

Carter formed the captive women in a small circle. Their children clung to their sides or sat on their knees. Ben Copeland appeared eventually, his haggard face attesting to the difficult time he'd had rooting the last Kwahadis from the boulders.

"I thought you dead," Copeland muttered. "And here you bagged the biggest bunch of all. Guess you'll want 'em taken north."

"They will be," Carter said, resting both his own rifle and the one snatched from Owl Eyes across one knee. "You're not arguing that, are you?"

"They're harmless enough," Copeland admitted. "That one at your side looks to 've ridden some, though."

"He has," Carter agreed. "Now he's in my care, though."

"You might devote your attentions to your own kind," Copeland growled. "Mullins got himself killed. The Pope boys, too. Barney McDowell has a bullet in one leg, and Hadley's caught one in the shoulder."

"He'll be all right?" Carter asked, his forehead wrinkling with concern.

"In time. Free him from chores for a while, I'd guess. I suppose your boy Brady could help him catch up with his lessons."

"I imagine Brady'd enjoy that."

"We killed four in the rocks. Together with the one you got at the far end of camp and the two down here at the creek, that makes seven. Two wounded ones in the camp. Plus captives. We've made a fair haul."

Yes, Carter thought. We've killed four men and three boys. We've created widows and orphans. A busy morning's work!

Carter gazed sadly at the frightened faces of the captives

as the ranchers dragged corpses from the rocks. Cooper McDowell carried the two boys from the creek. Loflin nudged the old woman and her charges along, and others brought additional captives to join Carter's batch down at the creek. The wounded warriors stared defiantly at their captors. The dead, joined at last by the boy Carter had killed, gazed lifelessly at the heavens.

"Which one is the Ghost?" Copeland asked the wounded Comanches.

Carter stepped out from the captives and attempted to blunt Copeland's anger.

"Can't you tell?" Carter asked, turning finally to look at the dead. He recognized several of the faces. Johnny was not among them.

"I think it's this one, Pa," Hadley said, pointing at a bullet-riddled corpse on the far right.

"Was that him?" Copeland asked the warriors. Carter's eyes pleaded for an answer. Both Kwahadis nodded, and Copeland yelled loudly. He then knelt beside the body and cut off its scalplock.

The others shouted their approval, and as if Copeland's actions removed the lid from a bubbling kettle, they set upon the bodies, stripping clothing and prying ankle bands and rings from stiffening legs and fingers. Only the boy at the far end and the two naked youngsters were spared. Carter guarded the first, and the others had nothing to rob.

"This is the white man's way I am to learn?" Owl Eyes asked when Carter returned.

"You're going to tell me Kwahadis never strip the dead?" Carter asked. He then whispered in Comanche words, "Our brother is not there."

Owl Eyes brightened, then turned and gazed at the distant hills and trees. Carter felt it, too. Somewhere, perhaps bleeding and certainly alone, Johnny watched it all.

"I can return to the old ways," Owl Eyes said.

"No, that truly is over," Carter said sadly. "Truly."

Owl Eyes's smile vanished, and the old sadness returned. But beneath it all Carter thought he detected a glimmer of hope, a sparkle of cheer.

CHAPTER 19

CARTER didn't have long to tend the captives. The shots had drawn the attention of the cavalry, and soon the young lieutenant appeared with his patrol.

"Looks like you got the job done after all," the lieutenant told Ben Copeland. "My compliments. Captain Kendall's camped back at the river. I'll send for some wagons. We'll soon have this group on their way to the reservation. They'll trouble you no longer."

"Two are wounded," Copeland pointed out.

"We'll see they get proper attention, though it's surely a waste. These Indians never seem to get well when they're captured. Where are the dead?"

Copeland led the way to the corpses. He took great pleasure in pointing out the infamous Gray Ghost.

"He'll haunt you no more," the lieutenant said, laughing. "Shame you scalped them, though. They would have made a fine showing. We have a photographer along. We could have taken their pictures."

"Those three at the end aren't cut up," Copeland declared.

"Well, I'd hardly want my Molly to think we made war on babies," the officer explained. "Why, those two you stripped are barely ten, I'd guess. If the New York press got wind of that, they'd fry us like slabs of bacon, likely have the Congress give the whole of Texas to Quannah Parker for Christmas. Best you bury 'em. I'll detail some men to help."

"We have three of our own to bury," Copeland objected, "and wounded to get to town. You want 'em buried, you do it. I'd as soon leave 'em to feed the buzzards."

"That's fine for the older ones, but you don't want those

boys out here for people to see," the lieutenant argued. "I'll have Sergeant Nettles pick a squad and get after it. You did our fighting. I guess we can do your burying."

Ben Copeland then turned over the captives to the soldiers and got Hadley mounted. The McDowell brothers had already departed. Mullins and the Pope brothers were taken to town. The other ranchers dispersed toward their homes.

Carter remained long enough to see the young Comanche wasn't disturbed by the soldiers. When the dead were buried, he prepared to lead Owl Eyes off. The lieutenant stopped that.

"This boy speaks good English," Carter explained. "I thought to take him in myself, raise him with my own boys."

"I'm afraid not," the lieutenant insisted. "He's my prisoner."

"He's thirteen years old," Carter argued. "He has no family. There's no one at the reservation to look after him."

"Somebody will," the lieutenant assured Carter. "You don't want to get mixed up with these young bucks, you know. They may seem as peaceful as doves, but believe you me, I've seen boys of his age shoot and scalp with the best of them."

"I'll be responsible for him," Carter declared.

"No, I'm the one who's responsible," the lieutenant countered. "My orders are clear. Every Kwahadi Comanche south of the Red River is to be delivered to Ft. Sill. You're not going to try and tell me he's just had a little bit too much sun?"

"It's all right," Owl Eyes said, gazing sadly up into the hills. "I go with my people."

"I'll be up there to get you," Carter promised.

"Yes," the boy said, mustering a distant smile. "We'll hunt the deer before the first snow comes."

"And I will teach you."

Owl Eyes then grew solemn. "Find him," the boy spoke in Kwahadi. "Don't let him die alone."

"I'll come before winter," Carter pledged again, nodding to reassure Owl Eyes that Johnny would be found.

A pair of wagons rumbled up the creek then, and soldiers began marching the captives in that direction. Owl Eyes stared reluctantly toward the creek, the rocks, and at Carter.

"Before winter!" Carter shouted.

Soldiers then led the boy away, and Carter wept inside. A month or two was an eternity at thirteen. Give him strength, Carter prayed. And give me eyes to find my brother.

CHAPTER 20

CARTER Ross climbed through the boulders above the creek. He looked past the nicks torn by rifle bullets, ignored the brass casings, and tried without success to avoid the bloodstained rocks and leaves. Scraps of deerskin, a moccasin, and the shattered shaft of a spear provided evidence of the battle fought there. No clue to Johnny's escape appeared, though.

Where have you gone, Johnny? Carter silently asked. How far could a hobbled, one-armed man get?

One with the heart of a mountain panther could make it to New Orleans and back if he had a mind, Carter told himself. So on he walked, though the going was hard, and the search was fruitless.

By the time the last of the soldiers had departed, the sun hung high and bright in the autumn sky. The burning lodges had been consumed, and the powder smoke had faded into memory. Birds now sang where hours before men had fought and died.

Time cures all, Carter told himself. But he wondered if it would mend the great tear in his heart or salve the wounded pride of the Kwahadis.

He found his first Comanche nestled in a crack between two large boulders. It wasn't Johnny. Carter knew instantly by the figure's short stature and stout body.

"You can come out," Carter called.

When there was no response, Carter touched the man lightly on the back. The skin was cold and stiff.

"Another corpse," Carter mumbled.

He paused long enough to pile a few rocks so that the

tomb was complete. Then he continued through the boulders.

Copeland'll be disappointed he didn't know about that one, Carter thought as he threaded his way through the treacherous ground. That makes eight. And maybe there are others.

There were. Carter located three of them. The last was still alive, and Carter ministered to the fatally wounded Kwahadi as best he could. The Indian's back was torn by bullets, though, and death's veil was already upon his eyes.

"Did you see my brother, Johnny Ross?" Carter asked as he let the Comanche sip water from a canteen. "I'm Carter. You remember me from the summer we rode together after buffalo. Johnny and I, we were Swallow's boys."

"Yes," the exhausted Kwahadi said, moaning. "Yes."

He died before saying another word, though, and Carter was once again on his own.

"Johnny?" Carter finally called out loudly. "Johnny?"

No one answered. Carter didn't know whether to rejoice that his brother had again escaped being among the dead or to cry because now the uncertainty had returned.

"Try to find the good among the bad," old Walt had often urged.

But walking those rocks, surrounded by the specters of dead Comanches, listening to the echoes of rifles resound through his head, Carter couldn't help wishing himself back home. By now word of the battle must have found its way up Ioni Creek. Hope would fret until he returned. The boys would wonder if their uncle remained alive, if Owl Eyes had been killed.

"Johnny, where are you?" Carter called.

His words echoed back to him in ghostly fashion, and for a moment Carter shook from head to toe. Then he regained his composure and left the rocks. His horse remained tethered a half a mile away, and he set off to retrieve it. As he passed through the embers of the Kwahadi camp, Carter began to notice a strangeness in the air. It was more than burning deerhide or charred yucca. No, his flesh tingled. He felt eyes on his back.

"Johnny?" Carter called again.

There was no answer this time, either, but as Carter's eyes examined the slopes, he detected signs of flight. Broken branches and upturned leaves hinted that someone had recently climbed the hill. Of course, Carter knew it might have been Copeland and the others attacking the camp. Something drew Carter in that direction, though.

The trail was a strange one. Blood stained the ground. One leg dragged behind the other.

"So, little brother, you're up here," Carter whispered. "Up here, waiting for me."

Carter didn't call out this time. He marched onward, ducking out of the way of branches and deftly avoiding the sharp spines of pencil cactus. The trail remained fresh and clear. Johnny hid no longer. He was in desperate flight, and the bleeding seemed to be worsening.

Carter trembled. He knew pain well. It was an old friend, and he wished he could somehow take Johnny's hurt upon himself. Once, when they were little, Carter had accepted blame for taking a stolen roll from a neighbor's kitchen. Johnny had snatched it, but Carter took the lashing that resulted. Afterward, though, Johnny had been the one to weep.

"I'm smaller," Johnny had said. "They wouldn't have hit me so hard."

"I'm older," Carter had answered. "I feel it less."

We're more than just brothers, Carter thought as he drew closer. The blood was fresh now. He could hear leaves rustling just ahead.

Our hearts are the same. And now I've brought on his death.

When Carter reached the crest of the hill, he found Johnny waiting, pistol in hand.

"I should've known," Johnny said, tossing the gun aside. "No one else would've stayed. I've cheated the soldiers, Cart. There's not blood enough left in me to reach the fort."

"Johnny?" Carter said, sitting beside his brother and examining a pair of bullet holes in Johnny's side. A half-hearted try at binding the wounds had barely slowed the bleeding.

"It's not that I mind dying so much," Johnny muttered. "I do wish I could see John Tyler grow tall."

Carter grinned. Johnny hadn't used J. T.'s entire name since the war.

"He has his mother's smile, but down deep that boy's you all over, Johnny," Carter said, easing a canteen to Johnny's lips. "I sometimes worry because there isn't much room these days for a maverick. But then I've always been a bit of one myself."

"Yes," Johnny mumbled, fighting to keep his eyes open. "Too much Kwahadi in your heart."

"I never should've let you leave Walt's."

"You couldn't stop me. Bound to happen, all this. Cart, I'd been no good on a reservation. Or raising horses, either. Walt knew that. You know it, too, down deep."

"You're the best man I know, Johnny."

"If I am, it's your doing. You raised me, Cart."

"No, we raised ourselves, we two. Old Walt and Swallow and Nighthawk had a hand in it, but we did most of the molding, I'd say. We always did have a way of finding our own path."

"Getting to the end of that path, brother."

"I know," Carter said, gripping Johnny's hand tightly.

"It's turned cold. Winter'll soon be here."

Carter frowned. The air was stifling hot. Death's hand had cold fingers, so it was said.

"I just . . . just wish . . ." Johnny stammered.

"Wish what?" Carter asked anxiously. "What?"

"Owl Eyes?"

"He's alive," Carter said. "Gone with the soldiers to the

reservation, but I swear to you, Johnny, I'll see he comes back here and lives with me."

"Yes," Johnny whispered.

For a moment Johnny's eyes closed, and a stillness settled over the hillside. Something thrashed around below. Carter readied his rifle, but when a large gray wolf appeared, he hesitated. The animal lifted his nose to the air and unleashed a great howl. It was answered by a second wolf and a third.

"They're calling me," Johnny said, reopening his eyes. "It's Nighthawk."

"No, wolves," Carter said, easing his brother's head onto one thigh. "Johnny, I can get you home. Hope can . . ."

"No, I hear the wolves," Johnny mumbled. "They're calling me."

"Just scavenging," Carter explained.

"You've forgotten so much," Johnny said, grinning. "Too much white skin. Blue eyes, too. Yellow hair. Nighthawk's father was a wolf, remember?"

"Wolf That Runs," Carter whispered. "I remember."

"Owl Eyes. He's the last . . . last of Nighthawk's blood . . . last of the wolves. There should be . . . something . . . something left of 'em."

"Yes," Carter agreed.

"When I'm . . . gone . . . give him my name. The others . . . all gone. Mother . . . father . . . brothers . . . all gone. Only you are left, Cart."

"And you."

"Not for long," Johnny said, coughing violently. "I can't cheat death. The wolves're calling. I can't . . ."

"Johnny, don't worry about Owl Eyes. I'll fetch him soon as I can."

"Yes," Johnny mumbled as blood trickled from the corner of his mouth. "Cart, it's so cold. You'll watch him come winter. He's awful thin just now, and . . ."

Those first words came like a torrent. Then the coughing resumed, and Carter tried to move Johnny so that the spasms would cease. Finally Johnny caught his breath and managed a faint smile.

"It'll be hard to grow tall in a land without buffalo." Johnny lamented, blinking his eyes to clear the tears. "You'll raise him?"

"As my own."

"Yes," Johnny said softly. "Teach him peace, Cart. Teach 'em all peace. War brings only the long death."

For a minute Johnny sat up. The coughing seemed to have cleared his chest. His eyes appeared alert and clear. A song rose from his lips—the death chant of the Kwahadi Comanches.

Johnny Ross never finished it. The wolves howled again, and Johnny stared at his brother. Life flowed from him like a cloud sent upon its way by a gentle autumn breeze. There was no convulsion of pain or cry of anguish.

"Go gently, little brother," Carter whispered. The wolves howled again, and Carter closed his brother's eyes. They're mourning the passing of an old friend, Carter thought. And I've lost a brother.

"It's bitter hard you leaving like this," Carter said, shuddering as he took Johnny's body in his arms and set off to locate his horse. "You're younger. I should've rested your sons on my knee as we rocked out the years of our old age. But Rosses don't live to see many sunsets, little brother. And now there's one less of us."

Carter found his horse where he'd left it. He tied his lifeless bundle on the nervous animal, then set off homeward. The ride took the balance of the afternoon, and he stumbled, hungry and exhausted, up to the house a little after dusk.

"Pa?" Brady called. "That you, Pa?"

"It's me," Carter answered, stumbling to the door. His shirt stained with Johnny's blood, Carter leaned wearily against the wall. His eyes were wide and red from exertion and lack of sleep. Brady helped him to a chair.

"Pa?" J. T. asked, scrambling over to examine the bloody chest for a wound.

"Outside," Carter mumbled. He then closed his eyes and passed from consciousness.

CHAPTER 21

WHEN he awoke, Carter found himself lying in bed, bathed and shaven. Rachel sat beside him, her bright eyes sparkling in the morning sunlight seeping in through the bedroom window.

"Little flower?" Carter said, fingering her silky hair. "It's morning? I've slept late."

"Ma?" Rachel called. "Pa's awake."

Hope raced into the room and sat beside him.

"I slept awhile," Carter mumbled.

"A full day and half of another," she told him. "You were half dead."

"Just half, though," Carter said sadly. "Not all."

"We saw Johnny," she said, kissing his forehead. "I wish it could've turned out differently."

"Was bound to be," Carter told her. "Still hurts, though."

"Reverend Hollings came by," Hope said, helping him sit up. "People in town have said prayers for you."

"For me?" he said. "Wasn't anything wrong with me."

"Nothing you couldn't shake anyway. Carter, you were a bit out of your head. You spoke of wolves and buffalo and little Owl Eyes."

"He's up at the reservation. I promised to bring him home."

"What?" she asked. "I don't understand."

"I promised Johnny I'd bring him home. I'd taken him with me straight off except some fool lieutenant dragged the boy along, saying all the Kwahadis belonged on the reservation. We'll likely have to file papers or some such nonsense."

185

"No, I think not," she said. "Owl Eyes is down at the corral helping Brady work the mustangs."

Carter grinned. The boy was indeed Johnny reborn.

J. T. and Nathan appeared in the door then, smiling like a pair of silver dollars at their father. Carter waved them inside, and the boys climbed up on the bed and settled each one under a weary arm. Rachel burrowed in beside them, and little Rich dashed in to join the brood.

"You're home, Carter," Hope announced.

"Yes," he agreed, wrapping his arms around the youngsters and squeezing first them and then their mother tightly. "It feels so wonderfully good, too."

"We're glad you're back," J. T. declared. "We saved some ham from breakfast."

"Biscuits, too," Nate added. "Want me to fix you a plate?"

"I'll help," Rachel offered.

Carter nodded, and the children raced off to the kitchen.

"There's something left to do, you know," Carter said, frowning heavily.

"Yes," Hope told him. "Say good-bye."

"It's strange," Carter said, shuddering. "I always figured I'd be the one to go first. I don't even know where to put him. With Pa and old Walt down by the creek? Or up on Antelope Mountain with Nighthawk?"

"He's with your father," Hope said, stroking his chest. "There was need of burying him. I feared visitors, and I knew you wouldn't like the thought of anyone dragging Johnny to the courthouse."

Carter shivered at the thought.

"We haven't read any words over him, though," Hope continued. "Owl Eyes sang, and J. T. carved Johnny's name on a plank. Still, we thought it best to wait for you before reading verse."

"Tell Brady and Owl Eyes we'll do it after I eat something."

"I'll get the children cleaned up a bit, too. Into their Sunday best."

"No, Johnny wouldn't think much of that," Carter objected. "He never took to preachers, and he couldn't abide stuffy clothes."

"No, he couldn't," she agreed. "You're right. They should go as they are, a little dirt in their hair, and a hole or two worn in their shirtsleeves or the knees of their britches. Johnny would understand . . . no, appreciate that."

Carter grinned, and she escorted him into the kitchen. By the time he'd finished his ham and biscuits, the others were gathered outside.

Carter carried the family Bible to the gravesite. Someone, probably Brady and J. T., had trimmed the grasses around the little cemetery. The picket fence was in need of a coat of paint, too, and Carter made a note to pick up some on his next trip to town.

"I'm not so good at verse readings," Carter declared, handing Hope the Bible. "My brother Johnny lies here. He wasn't much for words at all. He believed in feelings, and I want to tell all of you his last thoughts were for you. He talked of peace, and he urged me to teach you of it. I'll do my best.

"Johnny Ross didn't know a lot of peace in his life. He was part of two worlds bent on tearing at each other, and I guess you could say he got caught in the middle. He did his best, fought the good fight, and he will be remembered by those who loved him."

Carter knelt beside the mound of earth and touched the plank bearing Johnny's name.

"He wouldn't want much more said of him," Carter went on, coughing away a tear, "than that he rode straight, was true to his word, and never let the people he loved suffer on his account. A good man lies here, and my heart is heavy because of it. Rachel, boys, he told me it will be hard to grow tall in a world without buffalo. I say it'll be hard to laugh in a world without Johnny Ross. But we'll try because he'd want us to."

Owl Eyes chanted once more, and Carter reached out and linked hands with Hope and little Rachel. The others joined in a human chain that encircled the grave.

"Rest easy, Johnny," Carter whispered. "You're not forgotten."

Hope then led the children in the singing of a hymn. They each knelt as their father had and said a personal farewell. When Hope waved the others along to the house, Carter held Owl Eyes back.

"You're surprised to see me?" the boy asked.

"Some. But then bluecoat soldiers never could keep watch worth a nickel."

"I heard the wolves call," Owl Eyes explained. "They led me here."

"Home," Carter said, gripping the boy by the shoulders. "I made you a promise. I made Johnny a couple. You'll always have a home here."

"I know," the boy said, nodding his head sadly.

"It won't always be easy. It's hard giving up the old and taking on the new. You're strong of heart, though, so you'll manage."

"Yes, I must."

"Johnny said you should take his name. That's fitting. You've got so much of him in your eyes, your heart. The thing is, though, we've already got one John Tyler Ross running around this place. So I think you should take the Ross part and come up with another first name."

"Yes?"

"I thought something that sounds like Owl Eyes. Maybe Oliver."

"Oll-i-verrr," Owl Eyes said, pondering the name.

"It's a good name. I don't know what it means, but I've known a couple of good men who wore it proudly. One died beside me in Tennessee."

"Then it's a warrior name."

"Yes, but Oliver Ward had a heart that longed for peace. That's the part I'd have you remember best."

"Yes," the boy agreed. "So now I am Oliver Ross?"

"That's right. Why don't we go tell the others?"

Young Oliver nodded, and Carter led the way past the graves that would always help him remember the past and on toward the family that would forever keep him mindful of the future. He knew, watching the boy race toward the corral in moccasins, that young Oliver would face a difficult path. But then so must Carter Ross. The gap, after all, remained.

The fence, though, was gone, and fierce streams were often bridged.

I'll find a way, Carter silently promised. For all of us.

If you have enjoyed this book and would like to receive details of other Walker Western titles, please write to:

Western Editor
Walker and Company
720 Fifth Avenue
New York, NY 10019